CHARLIE'S BONES

A Mystery

by

L. L. Thrasher

A Write Way Publishing Book

Copyright © 1998, Linda Thrasher Baty

Write Way Publishing
10555 E. Dartmouth, Ste 210
Aurora, CO 80014

First Edition; 1998

ISBN 1-885173-47-4

1 2 3 4 5 6 7 8 9 10

For
Helen Clare Thrasher
and in memory of
William Walton Thrasher

Chapter One

I never would have found Charlie if I hadn't decided to put in a pool. An in-ground pool. Which means you gotta dig, right? So I signed a contract with Splash 'N Shine Pools and on the second Monday in April some guys with big ugly noisy machines showed up and started digging. And the first thing they did is, they dug up Charlie.

Charlie wasn't in what you'd call prime condition. Worse than skin and bones. Just bones, in fact. The workmen stopped working, the cops showed up, and some reporters trampled the ice plant. Fifteen minutes after the story broke, a guy from some Native American organization came by and carried on something fierce about the destruction of sacred ground until a woman who was a coroner or medical examiner or old bone expert or something told him the bones weren't more than thirty or forty years old. He lost interest then, which struck me as funny. I mean the bones could've still belonged to an Indian, couldn't they? But I guess you have to be an *antique* Indian to be important. Anyway, it was a real circus in my backyard for a while.

I guess I should explain how I happened to be putting in a pool in the first place. I mean, me? A pool? Yeah, *right*, Duke and Lady Dutton's daughter putting in a pool. How lah-didah. Duke and Lady aren't titles, they're names. Nicknames, actually. Duke's real name was David Wayne Dutton and Lady's real name was Lucille Louise Layman Dutton. But Duke and Lady were never called anything but Duke and Lady and I've always been called Lizbet, although it's Elizabeth Ann Dutton on my birth certificate. I was Lizbet Dutton for twenty-one years, then I married this guy named Tom Lange and I liked the sound of my name then—Lizbet Lange—so I kept it when we split up the next year.

It's my dead ex, old Tom Lange himself, who's to blame for the whole thing if you want to go back to prime movers. If he hadn't struck it rich before he died and if he hadn't been such a mean old bastard that he cut his first two wives and the five kids they had between them right out of his will and if he hadn't wanted to spite them all so bad that he left everything he owned to the truck-stop waitress he married on a dare when he was sixty-two and divorced a year later, well, none of this would've happened. And I never would've found Charlie. I don't know, maybe it was all for the best.

I didn't think that at first though, let me tell you. The first thing I thought was that I was going crazy. I mean, there I was, minding my own business, which was watching a bunch of strangers digging up my entire backyard, like maybe they thought I had a whole cemetery of bodies buried out there, when all of a sudden I felt this warm, *tingly* feeling and then this voice, low and real close to my ear, said, *"Hello, Lizbet."*

"Huh?" I said, and spun around and there was Charlie. Not exactly in the flesh, but there. This is the part that's hard to explain. I mean, the whole thing is hard to explain, but this part is a real bitch. Charlie was *there* but at the same time he wasn't *really* there. I don't mean it was like in the movies when you can see right through the ghost. I couldn't see through him. He looked solid, but he just wasn't really there. It was more like I wasn't seeing him with my *eyes,* I was seeing him with my *mind* and I don't know how to explain it any better than that.

Charlie was quite a sight, let me tell you. I mean, how many hippies do you see today, right? But there was Charlie, with a silver and turquoise peace symbol on his chest and a leather thong tied around his head like a sweatband and straight blond hair down past his shoulders and bell bottom jeans and a blue chambray work shirt with a fringed leather vest over it and leather Jesus sandals. I mean, really, a *hippie?* My *parents* were hippies.

The funny thing is, I wasn't scared. I did have a kind of funny *whoops* feeling in my stomach, the kind you get when you suddenly realize you're two weeks late and the big jerk hasn't called you in three weeks. But I wasn't scared. For one thing, Charlie was kind of drop-dead good-looking, if you know what I mean. He just plain didn't look scary. Besides, I think he hypnotized me or something. It was his eyes, bright blue and wide open and I couldn't stop staring into them.

"You don't have to talk out loud," he said. He was real close to me and I thought I almost felt his breath against my skin.

"I don't?" I said. My voice came out squeaky and thin, like I'd inhaled helium. "What do you mean?"

"Sorry, miss. What did you say?"

I turned around, real slow, like someone hit the super-slo-mo button. The speaker was a middle-aged guy in a suit. A cop. He was about ten feet away and was looking right at me. If he saw a hippie standing behind me, his face sure didn't show it. "I didn't say anything. I mean, I was talking to myself."

"Well, as long as you don't start answering," he said and grinned like he thought he'd said something real original.

Then he walked off to talk to some other guy in a suit. The backyard was *crawling* with guys in suits.

"You don't have to say anything out loud, you just have to think it. I'll hear you."

Oh, god, I thought, *I'm losing my mind.*

"No you aren't. I've been waiting a long time. How'd you find me? Planting a garden?"

The Splash 'N Shine guys had finally left after the cops told them they couldn't put the pool in until the investigation was complete. "A swimming pool," I said. "They were digging up the ground for a swimming pool."

"If you keep talking out loud, they'll really think you're crazy. Those are cops, aren't they?"

I opened my mouth to say yes, then closed it and thought: *"Yes."*

"I thought so. They're twenty-seven years too late."

"Who—" I took a deep breath. *"Who are you?"*

"You're getting the hang of it. My name's Charlie Bilbo."

"Bilbo?"

"No jokes, please. I've heard them all. You're talking out loud again."

"Sorry. I mean—" I took another deep breath and said in my mind: *"Sorry, it's like a lifetime habit, you know? I always talk out loud."* The only explanation I can think of for me standing there in my own backyard talking—or *thinking,* I guess—to a hippie named Charlie Bilbo who wasn't really there is that he had some kind of hypnotic power over me. I mean, it didn't really even seem very strange right then. Something about him struck me as strange though and in a second or two I figured it out. *"You don't sound like a hippie. How come you don't say 'groovy' and 'like wow'?"*

"I'm undercover."

"*Undercover? You mean—what? You don't want anyone to know you're a hippie? Check out the clothes, Charlie. They kind of like shriek hippie.*"

"*I'm a cop. I was working undercover when ...*" He gestured toward the mess in my backyard.

If you can whisper in your mind, I did it then. "*When you ... died?*"

"*When I was murdered.*"

I don't know why I reacted the way I did. I mean, what did I think? That he keeled over with a heart attack in my backyard and four feet of dirt drifted over him? *Somebody* had to put him there and people don't do backyard burials unless they're up to no good, at least not that I ever heard of. So I guess I already knew in the back of my mind that he was murdered. It's just that hearing it put into words kind of spooked me. So anyway what I did was, my voice went squeaky on me again and I kind of yelped "Murdered!"

"Yes, miss ... uh, *mizz*, that's what we think. Preliminary investigation suggests the deceased was shot in the back of the head."

I had spun around at the sound of the voice. It was the same guy who'd told me not to answer myself. I hadn't even realized anyone was nearby, but he was only a few feet away, standing with three other suits. "How awful," I said.

"The teeth are intact. Still, it's going to be hard to make an identification after all this time. Medical examiner estimates the body's been there for close to thirty years."

"His name's Charlie Bilbo." I couldn't help it, I just blurted it out without thinking. Major mistake, wouldn't you know.

The cop said "Charlie Bilbo?" like it was Greek or something. Then he repeated it like it meant something *real* important. He stepped closer to me, his eyes getting all squinty. "What do you know about Charlie Bilbo?" He was standing right in front of me and the other suits suddenly crowded around.

"Nothing," I said. "I don't know anything about him."

"You said Charlie Bilbo. Do you know Charlie Bilbo?"

"Um ... um ..." Jeez, I was about to wet my pants. All I could think of was that I hadn't paid that parking ticket I got last month. I turned toward Charlie. He was still there, but only for a second. He grinned at me, a little-boy grin, like he'd just put some plastic vomit in a strategic spot and was waiting for me to see it. Then he was gone. Just like that. No more Charlie. I looked at the cop again. "Um ... I'm ... psychic."

"What?"

"I'm psychic. A psychic. A medium. A spiritualist. I commune with the dead. I received a message: His name is Charlie Bilbo. It just *came* to me. From out of the blue."

There's nothing worse than being stared at by a cop who doesn't believe a word you're saying. I was being stared at by four of them. Oh, jeez, why didn't I pay that parking ticket? And what about my juvie record? It was sealed, wasn't it? Please, God, don't let them find out I was picked up for spray-painting a dirty word on a cop car when I was fifteen. And there was that little possession charge, but, jeez, I was a just a kid.

All of a sudden the suits hit me. I don't mean the guys in the suits hit me. The *suits* hit me. Oh, shit, *suits*. These weren't cops, not local cops. They were FBI. *FBI!* And they were all staring at me like I was holding a smoking gun. I felt like GUILTY was tattooed across my forehead.

"It just came to me," I said.

"Look, miss ... uh, mizz ..." He consulted a miniature notebook. "Ms. Lange." He got stuck there for a minute. After he flipped a couple pages in the notebook, he said, "You're the widow of Thomas R. Lange, is that correct?"

"He died of natural causes." Oh *god,* why did I say that? "I'm not a widow. We were divorced. Tom Lange and me. He left me his—" *fortune.* Jeez, don't tell them that. "This house. He left me the house. Three months ago. When he died. It was in his will. I decided to put a pool in. Maybe he would've put one in himself, but he only lived here for six months before he died and besides he joined the country club so he could go there to swim and stuff like that. I decided to put a pool in. I didn't know—"

"You didn't know what, Ms. Lange?"

"That he was there."

"Who?"

Somewhere in the back of my mind, I heard a loud clang, like a jail door slamming shut. *Why* didn't I pay that parking ticket? "The bones. I didn't know they were there."

"But you said they're Charlie Bilbo's bones. Isn't that correct?"

"Uh."

The suits exchanged a look. I didn't know what it meant, but I didn't like it. "Charlie Bilbo isn't dead, Ms. Lange. Not as far as anyone knows. He did ... uh ... leave the area abruptly back in the 'sixties, but we have every reason to believe he's alive. Have you been in contact with him?"

Now how was I supposed to answer that? And what did they mean he wasn't dead? I just *talked* to him, for chrissake. Of *course* he was dead. I couldn't think of anything to say so I took my mother's advice: *This liberated-woman crap is bullshit, Lizbet. When you're in a pickle, pull the old fragile-female trick. Works every time. Men are real suckers for it.*

I raised my left hand slowly to my forehead. "I ... I'm sorry. I feel ... faint." I let my knees buckle, like I was going to fall right down. Suddenly I had three or four suits herding me toward the house.

Right off the brick patio, which we walked across to get to the house, is a room that I don't really know the name of. There's a living room and there's a den and there's a family room and there's a library and there's a rec room downstairs, so what do you call *this* room? It's furnished like a living room, but whoever heard of two living rooms? I guess maybe it's the casual living room and the other one is the formal living room, but, jeez, talk about extravagance. I like this one best. It's all done in muted greens and blues and the furniture is covered with puffy mounds of pillows and the carpet is so soft it's like walking on water, only your feet don't get wet.

I sank back against the pillows of the couch and closed my eyes. When I opened them, they would all be gone. Wrong. Only one of them was gone and he showed up in a second with a glass of water. Actually, a crystal goblet of water. There ain't nothin' tacky in this house. Except for me.

I drank all the water, trying to stall for time, which was a big mistake because now I *knew* I was going to wet my pants if I didn't get to a bathroom in a hurry. I tried to figure out which one was the closest, in case I had to make a run for it. There are seven of them, in case you're wondering. Eight, if you count the one in the servant's apartment over the garage. "I don't feel good," I said.

"Maybe you should rest for a while, Ms. Lange. There will be some men out back for a few more hours. We need to return to the office, but when you're feeling up to it, call me. I want to hear what you know about Charlie Bilbo."

"I don't know anything about him. I just know his name."

He didn't answer. He handed me a card. FBI, just like I

thought. His name was Robert Martin. Sounded phony to me. "Look," I said, "the bones have been there for twe—" I almost bit my tongue off. It was Charlie who'd mentioned twenty-seven years. "Twenty-five or thirty years. Isn't that what you told me?"

"That's a fair estimate."

"Well, I'm only twenty-three years old. How would I know anything about a body that was buried before I was born?"

None of them came up with an answer. And then they all went away. I made it to the bathroom just in time.

Chapter Two

I was washing my hands when I realized what had happened. I'd hallucinated. That's all Charlie was, a hallucination. Probably caused by the shock of finding a skeleton where my swimming pool was supposed to be. Of course, I wasn't all that shocked when they found the bones. Surprised, for sure, but it wasn't like it was a fresh body dripping blood or anything. Mostly I was irritated. I was supposed to be getting a swimming pool and instead I got bones and cops and reporters. Now there might be a big delay and it could be August before I could swim in my very own pool.

A hallucination, that was all. But how did I know Charlie Bilbo's name? He was a real person. He had to be, because the suits recognized the name. I must have heard it somewhere. Maybe one of the cops had mentioned him and I just didn't remember overhearing it.

I dried my hands, then hung the little hand towel—which probably cost twenty bucks new—on the gold towel rack. Solid gold, maybe. I mean, who knows? The vanity countertop is marble. Marble! In a bathroom! I straightened the towel carefully, making sure the hems were even. All of a sudden I didn't want to leave the bathroom. What if he was out there?

"I'm right here."

I knew it a half-second before he spoke because I got that warm, tingly feeling again, only this time my knees went weak, too. "Oh, god," I said and sat down on the toilet. I never used to put toilet lids down but all the toilet seats in the house have lids made of fancy carved wood and they're so pretty it seems a shame not to be able to see them so now I keep the lids down all the time. So at least it wasn't as undignified as sitting on a toilet seat with the lid up.

Charlie was standing by the door. Which means he was about ten feet from me. You could hold parties in these bathrooms, no kidding.

"There's nothing to be afraid of, Lizbet."

"Yeah, right, I'm only talking to a ghost and the FBI's going to throw me in jail for killing you before I was born."

He smiled, not the little-boy grin, just a friendly smile. Suddenly, I felt calm again. "How do you—" *"How do you do that?"*

"You can talk out loud when no one's around if it's easier for you. How do I do what?"

"How do you fix it so I don't go right out of my mind? You're dead, for chrissake. You're a *ghost.*"

"I'm not sure. I don't understand how everything works. It's just the way it is. If I drove you insane, I couldn't get my work done, could I?"

"Work? What work? You mean you have a job? What do they pay you with? Oh, I get it, you have to earn your wings, is that it?"

"Not exactly."

"Do you *have* wings? When you're not here, I mean. When you're wherever you are when you aren't here."

"Sorry, that's classified information."

"Oh, shit. Heaven's a celestial Pentagon. Or are you from Hell?"

He smiled. A really great smile. Great shoulders, too. And long, long legs, and biceps ... Jeez, I was getting horny over a ghost. His smile broadened. Uh-oh.

"Um ... can you ... do you know what I'm thinking all the time?"

He just kept on smiling.

"Where were you? Where did you go?"

"I didn't leave. You just couldn't see me. I thought you'd be too nervous if you could see me."

I stood up and put my hands on my hips. "Did you watch me pee?"

"No. I promise. There are rules."

"Rules?"

"Rules ... I don't know how to explain it. I'm not a completely free agent. I can't do all the things I'd like to do."

What did that mean? That he would've liked to watch me pee? I sat down again and crossed my legs. I was barefoot and wearing blue jeans but they were like *beyond* designer jeans. I couldn't even pronounce the brand name, that's how French they were, and they cost more than I used to make in a week. And I had this silk shirt on, pale blue and so soft it was like being naked. Being rich is really something. I used to get most of my clothes at thrift shops. "You were murdered. Is that why you're here? To get revenge on your killer?"

"Revenge? No, I don't think it's anything like that. Revenge isn't important. I'm not sure why I'm here. I just know I am. There's some reason, though. There's a reason for everything."

"You don't know why you're here?"

"Not exactly. Maybe I'm supposed to clear my name. I was falsely accused. The matter was never cleared up. Oh, everyone will know the truth eventually. But not in this life and ... maybe it's important for them to know the truth now. I'd like to do that, clear

my name. I don't like thinking my friends and family and co-workers will go to their graves thinking I was evil."

Evil. It sounded so, well, *Biblical.* "I suppose it isn't very nice. To know they think that."

"No. Not nice at all. My wife took our son and moved away and changed her name. Out of shame. She was ashamed of me."

"You're married?"

Charlie laughed. A great laugh, free and wild and kind of joyful. *"Not now. Marriage is strictly an earthly convention. She divorced me anyway."*

"Because she didn't know she was a widow, right? The FBI guy said you aren't dead. As far as anyone knows."

"Yeah, no one knows I'm dead. They all think I absconded with a million dollars. We had a big bust set up, but it went wrong. They think I got away with the money and they think I'm still alive, living off stolen money. A good cop turned bad. But it didn't happen like that. I was a good cop all the way. I was murdered and it was set up to look like I grabbed the money and ran."

"So ... is it all over now? They'll identify your body. They'll know you were killed so you couldn't've stolen the money, right? It'll all be over then, won't it?"

"I don't think it's going to be that easy. I'm not sure what's going to happen, but if it were that simple, I wouldn't be here. You would have dug your pool anyway and they would have found me. Something else is going to happen. I don't know what, but there's a reason I have to be here. And there's something you have to do. Otherwise, you wouldn't know I was here."

"But ... what do I have to do? I mean, don't you have, I don't know, some kind of power or something so you can fix it so it comes out right?"

"I don't have any power. I can't change things or make things happen."

I thought about that for a minute. "But you did change things. You told me your name and I told it to the FBI and that changed things."

"What I meant was, I can't change things directly. I can only work through an agent."

"So I'm your agent?"

"It looks that way. The choice wasn't mine."

"Well. Gee. A ghost's agent. I'm a ghost's agent. It isn't going to be dangerous, is it? Whatever I have to do? I mean, jeez, this is about stolen money and murder."

"I don't know. I can't see the future, either."

Now *that* was real reassuring, let me tell you.

"Charlie?"

"Yeah?"

"Maybe I already did my part. Maybe they wouldn't have identified you for some reason. Maybe all I had to do was mention your name so they'd compare your dental records with your ... um ... the skeleton's teeth. Maybe if I hadn't told them your name, they'd never know it was you. So maybe it's all over, huh?"

"Maybe. But I don't think so." He grinned at me and said, *"I don't think the fun has even started yet."*

Fun? I thought of the hard, squinty-eyed looks the cop gave me. "Charlie," I said, "if this is supposed to be fun, trust me, it definitely hasn't started yet."

Chapter Three

We stayed in the bathroom for a few more minutes, Charlie just standing there by the door and me sitting on the toilet, trying to do some arithmetic in my head. If Charlie hadn't been there I would have written the numbers in the air, which always helps, but I had to settle for writing teeny-tiny numbers on the leg of my jeans, with my left hand sort of cupped around my right so he wouldn't know what I was doing. I finally figured out that twenty-seven years ago was 1969.

I know all about 1969. I don't mean I remember it, of course. I wasn't even born. But Duke was a real history buff and in the evenings he'd sit out on the back porch, tilting an old wooden kitchen chair back against the wall and propping his feet up on an upside down paint can, and he'd roll one of those funny cigarettes that Lady made him stop smoking the year I started high school and I would sit down on the porch step and he would talk to me, and what he talked about was history. Sometimes it was stuff he actually remembered—the years he lived through, you know—but other times he'd tell me about the Civil War or the 1920s or the Russian Revolution or whatever he felt like talking about.

Sometimes he let me choose: *Pick a year, Lizbet, any year. Nineteen sixty-nine? Well, let's see:* Midnight Cowboy *won the*

Academy Award for Best Picture; Best Actor went to John Wayne for True Grit, *Best Actress to Maggie Smith for* The Prime of Miss Jean Brodie. Easy Rider *and* Butch Cassidy and the Sundance Kid *were the best movies that year, if you ask me, although the Duke did a damn good job in* True Grit. *The Fifth Dimension won the Grammy for best record for "Aquarius." Best Album went to "Blood, Sweat, and Tears," an album by—guess what group, Lizzy-Lou.*

Blood, Sweat, and Tears, I answer and Duke roars with laughter. *You got it, baby. Lots of other good music that year, too: "Leaving on a Jet Plane" by Peter, Paul, and Mary, lots of other good songs. Okay, what else?* The Godfather *and* The Andromeda Strain *were on the bestseller list. "Sesame Street" debuted on television. New York and Baltimore were in the Super Bowl and the World Series. The Jets beat the Colts sixteen to seven, and the Mets beat the Orioles four to one. Hurricane Camille wreaked a little havoc all the way from Louisiana to Virginia. Nixon and the Soviets had the first of the SALT meetings. That's Strategic Arms Limitation Talks, Lizzy, supposed to lead to detente. You know what detente is?*

No, I say, and Duke laughs again and blows me a kiss. History was the only subject I never had any trouble with in school. I already knew it all. I still know it. I know *who, what, when,* and *where,* at least, but I don't really understand the *why* of most of it. But I get all the history questions right on *Jeopardy!*

Nineteen sixty-nine was one of Duke's favorite years. He'd talk about it for hours. *LBJ—that's Lyndon Baines Johnson, Litty-Bit, thirty-sixth president of the U. S. of A.—old LBJ couldn't stand the heat and decided to get out of the kitchen. The whole country was being torn apart by the War. Hell, the whole world. So Johnson says, "I shall not seek, and I will not accept, the nomination of my party for another term as your president," and the Democrats put Hubert Humphrey on the ticket. He lost, and come January, 'sixty-nine,*

Tricky Dick Nixon got himself sworn in. Old Ike died that year, too, couple months later, March, I think. He was an old coot by then, but I always thought his timing was good. He didn't have to watch his Veep fuck up the whole country.

Watch your language, Duke honey. Lady is standing inside the screen door, looking out and frowning at the joint Duke holds between his thumb and index finger.

There were over five hundred thousand U. S. troops in Vietnam in 'sixty-nine. Nixon ordered a withdrawal in May, and they started coming home in July, but it wasn't 'til 'seventy-two that Henry Kissinger told the world that "peace is at hand," and Nixon said we'd have "peace with honor" real soon. That was in October of 'seventy-two, just before the presidential election in November. Funny coincidence, huh? Great timing. Nixon got himself re-elected, then got himself in a whole heap of trouble and ended up resigning in August of 'seventy-four, only U. S. president ever to resign in disgrace.

Everyone was protesting back then, Lady says. *There were sit-ins and demonstrations at all the colleges. They sent the National Guard to Berkeley because the students wanted to name a piece of college land "People's Park." Sent a bunch of soldiers in over nothing but the name of a—*

That wasn't what it was about, Lady. It was about the War. It was all about the War. Nineteen sixty-nine: That was the year we went to Woodstock, Lizzy-bet, August of 'sixty-nine. Damn, what a weekend! Jimi Hendrix and Jefferson Airplane. The Grateful Dead. Judy Collins. Neil Young. Janis Joplin. We saw Joplin, me and Lady did, a couple years before that at the Monterey Pop Festival and that was why I really wanted to go to Woodstock—to hear Joplin sing again. Her voice ... Hell, you can't describe her voice with words. Remember that song we were listening to the other night, Lizzy-bet? "Me and Bobby Mcgee"? That was Janis Joplin. Kris Kristofferson wrote the song, but nobody'd even remember it now if Joplin hadn't sung it.

Can we go see her sing sometime? I ask and Duke shakes his head and says, *No, baby, she's not around anymore. Died the year after Woodstock, on the fourth of October in nineteen seventy. She was only twenty-seven years old, same age Jim Morrison was when he died, and Jimi Hendrix, too. Members of the Twenty-Seven Club. Damn shame she died. Joplin—they called her Pearl, you know; that was her nickname—she's singing with the angels now and I bet Heaven's really rocking.* Duke takes a quick drag on his joint and blows a smoke ring for me. *Sha-Na-Na. Arlo Guthrie. Ravi Shankar. Everyone was at Woodstock. Nothing like that before and there won't ever be nothing like it again. God, what a weekend.*

I had blisters on my heels, Lady says through the screen door, *and they hurt the whole time we were there, kept breaking open and bleeding. We walked the last ten miles or so, Lizbet. The people we caught a ride with started dropping acid and I got scared and made Duke tell them to stop and let us out as soon as we got to Woodstock—the town, I mean. Only it turned out that wasn't where the festival was. It was closer to a town called Bethel and we had to walk. I never walked so far in my whole life and by the time we got there I had to pee so bad my eyeballs were floating and I ended up going in the bushes because there weren't enough toilets and I couldn't wait.*

Creedence Clearwater Revival was there, Duke says, his voice thick with pot and nostalgia, *and the Who. They were all there. Hendrix, of course. He played "The Star-Spangled Banner" on Monday morning, the last day of the Festival. People were already leaving by then but we stayed 'til Hendrix finished playing. That song never sounded as good as it did with Hendrix playing it on a screaming electric guitar out there in that muddy field. God, there'll never be anything like it again. Best time there ever was.*

I stood up suddenly, not wanting to think about Duke and Lady anymore, and walked toward the door and Charlie turned and opened the door and walked out of the room. I stopped like I'd walked into an invisible wall. *Charlie opened the door and walked out.* Only he didn't really. I mean, he did. He opened the door. I saw him do it. Only it was like there were two doors all of a sudden, two doors in exactly the same place. I saw him open one door and walk out, but the other door, the *real* door stayed closed and it was *still* closed, but I could see Charlie because he hadn't closed the other door, *his* door, and it was still open and he was standing in the hall. On the other side of the real door. Which was closed. I could see into the hall but the door was closed. My mind kind of boggled, if you know what I mean.

"*Are you coming, Lizbet?*"

Under other circumstances, I might have made a snappy comeback to that—something real suggestive, if you catch my drift—but right then I was feeling just a little shaky. I took a step forward and opened the door—the *real* door—and it kind of blended into Charlie's door when the two of them were open the same distance and then there was only one door. Which was a real improvement, as far as I was concerned. I mean, a ghost *man,* all right, I can deal with that. But a ghost *door?*

I smiled at Charlie, only even I could tell it was a sick smile. "Can't you walk through walls?"

"*Why would anyone want to walk through a wall?*"

I couldn't think of an answer to that. I mean, why *would* you want to walk through a wall if there's a perfectly good door right there? So anyway, Charlie and me—pardon me, Charlie and *I*—I've been working on my grammar so the salesladies down at Madam and Eve's Boutique where I get most of my clothes don't smirk so much when I walk in. Where was I? Oh, yeah, Charlie and *I* walked down the hall and back into the muted blue and green whatever-room-it-is.

The crystal goblet was still on the end table so I picked it up and trotted off to the kitchen. I was going pretty fast. I had this real urgent need all of a sudden to get away from Charlie. I also felt like I was going to start crying. And I don't mean a few little tears. I felt like I was going to full-out bawl my head off.

I didn't get away from Charlie, though. He was right there behind me. I put the goblet down on the counter—this kitchen's got miles and miles of counter—and I turned around and there was Charlie. I felt a tear dribble down my cheek and thought, oh, shit, here I go. Then Charlie said my name. Just *Lizbet* real quiet and all of a sudden I felt calm, and I mean *really* calm, like I was tranked on something.

"Are you okay?"

"Yeah. I'm fine. It was just, for a minute there ... I mean, that thing with the door ..."

"Think of it as parallel universes. That's as close as I can come to explaining it. I can't actually touch anything in your world, or move anything, or pick anything up." He grinned. *"No hat floating up to sit on an invisible head or anything like that."*

I nodded. Parallel universes. Okay, I could handle that. And the funny thing is, I really could. That door thing really threw me for a loop for a minute, but now I was fine. I mean what's wrong with a ghost door, after all? A ghost door for a ghost. Why not?

All of a sudden, I was hungry. *Starving.* Which I guess isn't surprising since the Splash 'N Shine guys showed up at eight and, what with all the commotion, I hadn't even eaten breakfast and it was after one o'clock now. "I'm hungry," I said. "Are you hungry? Uh ... Do you eat?"

"I don't have to eat."

"But you can? Um, how about grilled cheese? I haven't been to the grocery store lately. I'm out of almost everything."

"Anything is fine."

I got the cheese and bread and butter out and found the cheese slicer. Charlie said, *"Just make however much you plan to eat."*

I tried not to think about that too hard. I made one grilled cheese sandwich and Charlie and I both ate it. We also drank the same glass of milk. It was actually kind of funny. Charlie picked up the sandwich and took a bite and he was holding it in his hand when I picked it up off the plate and took a bite. Parallel universes. Right. A real sandwich for me and a ghost sandwich for Charlie. It makes perfect sense, if you think about it. It hadn't even bothered me very much when Charlie sat down at the counter beside me.

He had pulled out one of the tall stools to sit on. Of course, the *real* stool didn't move, only his ghost stool did. Actually, seeing two stools kind of overlapping because they were taking up some of the same space made me feel like I was cross-eyed. I mean, two things can't be in the same space, right? Everyone knows that. It's some scientific thing, like how if you fill the bathtub too full and get in it, some of the water slops over the side because you and the water both take up space. And you can't have two things in the same space. There's probably a name for it. Somebody's Law or something like that. Duke and Lady were right—I never should have dropped out of school. Anyway, looking at the stool made me a little queasy so I didn't look at it any more than I could help.

Charlie drained the last of the milk from his glass—my version of the glass was still half full—and said, *"You need to call the FBI agent."*

"Later, okay? If I try to talk to him now I'll probably throw up my sandwich."

Charlie nodded. While I finished my sandwich, I found

myself staring at the peace symbol laying against Charlie's chest. It didn't look like homemade hippie shit, like the stuff I have in a box that belonged to Duke and Lady. I used to tell them they should throw all that old junk out but they said it had sentimental value and I guess it does because I sure can't bring myself to throw it out now.

Charlie's peace symbol did look handmade, just not cheap. The circle and the rocketship shape inside it were hammered silver. Five turquoise stones were set into the circle of silver, one at the top and the other four spaced evenly around it. If you wanted to, you could draw a star by drawing a line connecting the stones. Maybe that was symbolism. Although I couldn't think of anything a star symbolized, hippie-wise.

"That's really a nice pendant, Charlie. It doesn't look like all that cheap hippie junk people had in the 'sixties."

"The man who made it gave it to me. His name was Horst Martinez. German mother, Mexican father. He taught at Oak Valley College. I met him when his sister's husband was murdered. He wasn't well known then, but I think he was on the way. His work was written up in an art magazine a few months before I died."

I was sitting there with my mouth hanging open. Which Charlie eventually noticed. He said, *"What?"*

"That's a *Horst Martinez?* My god, Charlie, it's worth a fortune! He's ... he's, like one of the most famous artists in the country. I mean, I know about him and I don't know *anything* about art. There's a book in the library with pictures of his stuff. You want to see it?"

"Right now? Okay, but call the FBI before we leave."

"Not that library. *My* library."

Charlie followed me to the library, which is actually a fairly small room for this house, so it seems almost cozy. Bookshelves line three walls and a stone fireplace takes up the fourth. The bookshelves only go up about six feet, so you can reach the books on the top shelf easily. On the ledge that forms the top of the bookshelves are bronze busts, abstract metal sculptures, fancy vases, ceramic birds. There was an appraisal form with the papers the lawyer gave me. Some of those knickknacks are worth thousands of dollars.

The books look like they were ordered from the factory, or wherever you order books from when you just want to fill up some shelves. Most are classics, Shakespeare and stuff like that. The rest are the kind of books Lady called "artsy-fartsy books," big slick-looking volumes on art and history and collectibles. I've spent a lot of lonely evenings flipping pages in the library since I moved in.

I pulled *The Art of Horst Martinez* from one of the shelves and handed it to Charlie. He took it, but of course I was still holding it—life with a ghost is complicated—so I put my copy back on the shelf. Charlie took his book to the desk and sat down in the swivel chair. I curled up in one of the big armchairs and watched Charlie as he looked through the book. After a few minutes, he said, *"Look at this, Lizbet."*

I walked over to the desk and looked over his shoulder. And I couldn't see a damn thing on the page. I don't mean it was blank. It was like I could *almost* see something on the page, but not quite. I guess it was more like I could see the picture, I just couldn't comprehend it. *"You'll have to get your copy. Page thirty-seven."*

I got the book—the real book—off the shelf and opened it up next to Charlie's ghost book. Page thirty-seven was a color photograph of Horst Martinez, a candid shot taken in his studio. He was sitting on a tall stool at a workbench. The picture was taken from off to one side and Martinez appeared to have just turned toward the photographer. He had a surprised expression on his face, as if he'd been caught unaware. He looked more like a Martinez than a Horst, with darkish skin and black hair streaked a little with gray, and brown eyes. He was wearing jeans and a blue work shirt and worn-looking leather boots. A silver and turquoise peace symbol hung around his neck.

"He must have made another one for himself," Charlie said. *"He really hit the big time, didn't he? If I'd lived, I could have sold it for a small fortune. Some of his things have sold for hundreds of thousands of dollars."* Charlie sounded wistful. *"Damn, I would've been rich."* He flipped through some more pages in his book, then closed it and sighed. *"Sometimes I think it would be better ..."*

"What, Charlie?"

"If I hadn't come back."

"Did you have a choice?"

He gave me a strange look and said, *"I'm not sure."*

"Well. You can't sell your peace symbol since nobody can see it, so I guess you'll just have to go on being an underpaid undercover cop ghost."

Charlie laughed. God, his laugh was something else, so pure and joyful. I wondered if he'd laughed like that when he was alive. Then I had this sudden horribly intense aching kind of feeling and I wished I'd known him when he was alive. I wished I could touch him and brush back the blond hair from his cheek and ... Oh, god, somebody *killed* him.

"What's wrong, Lizbet?"

"Nothing."

"You're crying."

"No I'm not. I never cry." I turned my back to him and brushed away the tears and turned back and gave him a big smile. He didn't smile back. Instead he said, *"You better call that FBI agent."*

"Shit. What am I going to tell him?"

"Stick with the psychic story. There's no way he can disprove it."

"He'll think I'm nuts."

"Probably. But he'll also make damn sure the teeth are compared to my dental records."

"Yeah, I guess so. And that's what you want, right?"

Charlie nodded. We went back to the kitchen because I'd left the guy's card on the counter. I didn't really want to call him, so first I finished the last of my milk and cleared the dishes away. The dishwasher was only about half full and I'd been working on this load for a week. I only run it when it gets full and I don't eat in much, unless I order out for pizza or Chinese and then I use paper plates. And plastic forks. They look real tacky in the drawer next to the silverware. And I mean *silver*ware.

"Why don't you have a cook?" Charlie asked, which kind of made me wonder if he wasn't lying about not being able to read my mind all the time. I decided I was really going to watch what I was thinking from now on.

"I'd feel stupid having someone wait on me. I'm like *real nouveau* stinking rich. Up until three months ago I was a waitress at a truck stop."

"You inherited the money, right? From your ex-husband."

"The money, the house, the cars. There's a boat but I haven't even seen it yet. *Tons* of money, trust me. It takes a little getting used to. I keep checking out the grocery coupons in the newspaper. Like I really need to save a quarter on a bottle of ketchup, right?" I sat back down beside him, swiveling my stool to face him.

"Tom—that's my ex, Tom Lange—he wasn't rich when I was married to him. He was just this old retired guy who used to hang around the truck stop. Then all of a sudden he was filthy rich. See, what happened is, he used to work for some computer company. And while he was working there, he invented some kind of little gizmo that makes PCs able to process things like a million times faster, you know? He didn't get any money for it, though. But everyone used it. I mean there's one of his little gizmos—a chip or something, I don't know what it is—in every home computer ever made in the last ten or fifteen years. The whole computer industry practically exists because of this whatever-it-is Tom invented. Anyway, he thought he kind of got ripped off so he asked this lawyer to see what he could do and the guy took the case on a contingency basis and it took him years and years, but sonovabitch if he didn't win. Every computer manufacturer in the whole world had to pay Tom something for every single one of those little things in every single computer they ever made. It's kind of sad though because Tom died about six months after he got the money. His heart. He had a bad heart for years. I was always a little nervous that he was going to keel over dead while we were— Never mind. I'll make the call now."

I used the phone in the little office by the kitchen. I think it's for the cook to work out the menus or something like that. A woman with a whiny voice answered by repeating the phone number, like maybe I didn't know what number I called.

"Is Robert Martin there?"

"Who's calling, please?"

"I am."

"Your name, please?" I could almost hear her grinding her teeth.

"Lizbet Lange."

"One moment, please."

It was only a moment, too, a real quick moment, like maybe old Robert Martin was real anxious to talk to me. The funny thing is, he didn't ask me any questions. He just told me a couple things and then he said my backyard would remain cordoned off as a crime scene and some cops would be working out there for another day or two but after that I could go ahead and have the Splash 'N Shine guys come back to work. And then he said goodbye and hung up.

I put the receiver down and looked at Charlie. "Did you hear that?"

"No magic powers, remember?"

"First off, he said the case has been returned to the jurisdiction of the local authorities. I guess that means it turned out not to be the FBI's business, right?"

Charlie nodded. *"Yeah, I don't know why they were here anyway. Must've been hoping it was related to one of their cases. What else?"*

"He said he told the local cops about me saying the bones were yours and they already had your dental records in their files so the coroner or somebody did a rush job and compared them."

"And?"

"He said they don't match. He said the skeleton isn't yours."

Charlie didn't say anything for a long time. He just stood there looking at me, but I didn't think he was really seeing me. When he finally did say something, all he said was: *"Bummer."*

Chapter Four

It was almost four o'clock that afternoon when Charlie
and I got in the Porsche and headed off to the police station
in downtown Oak Valley.

Oak Valley is inland from San Francisco. Well, I guess you
can't very well be *out*land from San Francisco, can you? Unless you're on a boat. Anyway, a long time ago Oak Valley was
off by itself in its own pretty little valley, but now it's nothing
but urban sprawl in this part of California and you can drive
from my house, which is on the east side of Oak Valley in the
foothills of the Diablo Mountains, all the way to San Francisco, which is close to seventy miles away, without ever being
out in the country. It's just one town after another with nothing but malls and electronics plants separating them.

I moved to Oak Valley when Tom died and left me the
house. Before that I lived in San Jose for a while. And before
that I lived in Gilroy, Garlic Capital of the World. That's
where I was born and raised. Duke and Lady also grew up in
Gilroy but they were going to San Jose State University, which
was San Jose State College back then, and they were living in
a hippie crash pad with a bunch of other hippies when Lady
realized she was pregnant. The way Duke put it was Lady

suddenly got a bad attack of the nesting instinct. What she actually did was panic.

There she was, pregnant and not married and living in a ramshackle old house with a bunch of people who were usually stoned and someone was always having a bad trip and even with a dozen or so people sharing the house they always had a hard time coming up with the rent money and it dawned on Lady that maybe that wasn't a real good environment for a pregnant woman, let alone for a baby.

So Lady cried and carried on and Duke said *Oh, hell* and married her and got a job at the cannery in Gilroy where his father worked and they moved down there and rented a little house and after I was born Lady went to work at the same place and she worked swingshift and Duke worked days until I started to school and then they both worked days and everything was pretty normal. But they were always hippies at heart. Until the day they died they talked about Woodstock like it had happened yesterday.

Sometimes it seems to me that the history Duke told me about always had to do with people dying. I guess that's what history is, a long story about people who died. History's full of people dying before their time, too—JFK and his brother Bobby, Martin Luther King, Jr., Abraham Lincoln, even Jesus Christ. It sure seems like you have a better shot at getting in the history books if you die young.

Nineteen sixty-nine was full of people dying. People were starving to death in Biafra, and the Arabs and Israelis were killing each other just like always, and the British and Irish were going at it in Belfast just like always, too. King Saud of Saudia Arabia died. Soldiers were dying in Vietnam, and the president of North Vietnam, Ho Chi Minh, died, although he died of old age, not the war, and him dying didn't change anything. The war just kept on going on.

Celebrities died in '69, too. I remember Duke talking about them: *Janis Joplin,* he says and sighs. *Boris Karloff. Brian Jones. He was a guitarist with the Rolling Stones, but he didn't make the Twenty-Seven Club, didn't live long enough. Some people thought Paul died— that's Paul McCartney, one of the Beatles, Lizbet—but he didn't. It was just a rumor going around because some fool played a record backward and thought it sounded like it was saying "Paul is dead."*

Lady says, *The Smothers Brothers television show died in 'sixty-nine, and so did the* Saturday Evening Post. They laugh about that, but I don't understand how a TV show can die and I don't know what the *Saturday Evening Post* is.

Judy Garland—wasn't that the same year, Lady? Duke asks and Lady nods her head even though Duke isn't looking at her and he goes on: *You know who she is, Lizzy-bit. The little girl in* The Wizard of Oz. *We watched it on TV just last spring, remember?* I get teary-eyed at the thought of Dorothy dying, so Duke says, *"Now, now, Litty-bitty, she wasn't a little girl when she died. The movie was made way back in the 'thirties, nineteen thirty-nine's when it premiered. Judy Garland was way older than I am when she died.*

You aren't going to die, are you, Duke?

He laughs and says, *Not for years and years and years, Libby-Lib.*

I believed him. But he was wrong. He died before his time and so did Lady.

I don't like to think about the way they died. Talk about senseless deaths. See, after I quit school and moved out of the house, they put a down payment on a piece of land west of Gilroy and they bought an old camp trailer and spent the weekends there building a house. The house was coming along pretty good but they were still living in the camp trailer three years ago in February when there was a real cold snap. Not forty below or anything like that, but even a few degrees below freezing is pretty rare in this part of the state. Anyway, Duke and Lady left an old space heater on when they went to bed and carbon monoxide built up in the trailer and by morning they were dead. A friend of theirs from work drove down to see what was wrong when they didn't show up for work Monday morning. They were both forty-three years old. I don't like to think about it.

I brought the Porsche—bright red and flashy as anything—to a stop at a traffic light about a block from the police station and said, "Listen, Charlie, I don't really want to do this."

"So you've said. About a hundred times."

"Well, why don't you listen? Cops scare the hell out of me."

"Why? Are you a criminal?"

"Of course not. It's just ... they make me feel guilty."

"You'll do fine."

"No, I won't. I'll screw it all up. I know I will. I always screw everything up. I wasn't even a very good waitress because I used to mix up the orders. I'd give some guy a chili dog when he ordered a chili burger and stuff like that. Truckers are nice guys though and I always remembered their names and flirted with them a little so they gave me good tips anyway. But *cops.*"

"There's a parking place. Try to remember not to talk out loud if there's anything you want to say to me while we're in there, okay?"

I pulled the car into the parking spot and shut off the engine and Charlie and I both got out. Charlie went up the steps ahead of me and went inside. His door hadn't even closed all the way when I opened the same door and walked inside. For a second I had the weird feeling that his door was going to hit me in the face when it closed but it didn't. It just sort of faded away. All of a sudden I wondered what would happen if I tried to touch Charlie. I'd been real careful not to get too close to him because, to tell the truth, the thought of touching a ghost was just a little too creepy to even think about.

He was reading a sign by the elevator when I caught up with him. "Jeez, do you have to walk so fast?"

A cop in a uniform, who was also waiting for the elevator, gave me a sharp look. Shit. I was talking out loud.

"If they put you in a strait jacket, I can't get you out," Charlie said.

"All right, all right, I'll try to remember."

"We need to go to the third floor."

The cop seemed to have second thoughts about getting in an elevator with a crazy woman, so we had it all to ourselves. "Listen, Charlie, why can't you just find out what you want to know by reading minds? I could just toss out a question or two to be sure they're thinking about you and you could read their minds."

"I can't read minds."

"What do you mean? You read mine, right?" I took a deep breath and thought: *"I'm not talking out loud now and you know what I'm thinking."*

"Yeah, but you're making a conscious effort to communicate with me. You know I'm here. No one else does. You're the one I'm supposed to use."

Use? I didn't much like the sound of that.

The elevator doors slid open and we stepped out on the third floor. *"Sometimes you seem to know what I'm thinking about when I'm not trying to communicate with you."*

"I do that the same way you do: body language, facial expressions. You have a very expressive face, Lizbet. And a very pretty one."

Jeez, I was being hit on by a ghost.

Charlie grinned at me. *"That wasn't a pass, just an honest opinion."*

And he claimed he couldn't read my mind!

"Homicide division's down this way." He gestured to the left. *"How do you know? This building's only about two years old. The old police station's the city museum now."* He pointed to a sign by the elevator doors. Little red arrows pointed the way to various departments.

"I hate a smartass ghost," I told him, and headed down the hall.

I had to explain to two or three people that I wanted to talk to someone about the skeleton in my backyard before a uniformed cop who kept hitching up his belt, which must have weighed about thirty pounds what with the gun and all the other cop stuff hanging from it, led me to be a tiny, stuffy cubicle. The guy behind the desk looked familiar, so I was pretty sure he'd been at my house that morning. I hadn't paid all that much attention to them.

The name plate on the desk said he was Captain John Sterling. He was in his late forties and looked a little bit like Sean Connery, but not as sexy. He told me to have a seat, which I did, carefully smoothing my skirt over my legs. I'd changed clothes because I figured if I couldn't dazzle them with brilliance I could at least intimidate them with wealth.

I'd chosen a silk suit in light peach with an even lighter peach blouse under the jacket, and shoes and a handbag that were soft peach leather, dyed, I guess, since I've never heard of a peach-colored cow. Lady taught me years ago that makeup is supposed to be subtle and I never have a bad hair day, at least not since I started paying a hundred bucks a clip down at Coiffures By Monsieur Jacques. It's my real color—a funny reddish blond—and has just enough natural curl to give it some bounce and Jacques himself fixed me up with a real swingy style that comes just to my chin and is cut in a bunch of layers or something so it's nice and full and just falls right back into place if I shake my head or go out in the wind or something. I'm a real class act. Until I open my mouth.

"What can I do for you, Ms. Lange?"

"Well, Captain," I said and gave him my dimpliest smile, like meeting a real live *captain* was the highlight of my drab life. "It's just that I'm a little upset about having a skeleton show up in my backyard and I wondered if you've identified him yet."

"No, Ms. Lange, we haven't. Identification of skeletal remains can take a long time. We might have to compare the teeth with dental records from every known missing person in the state before we come up with a match and even then we may never find a match at all. There's no reason for you to concern yourself with it. The body had been there for twenty or thirty years, long before you had any connection with the property."

"But I know who he is. It is. The skeleton. I know whose bones they are."

"So I understand, Ms. Lange. The FBI told me you claimed to be psychic." He leaned toward me, clasping his hands on the desk. He gave me a real earnest look. Real earnest and phony as hell. "Charlie Bilbo isn't dead and those aren't his bones. I don't know how you came up with his name but I'd like you to tell me. How do you happen to know him? Or know about him."

"I ..." I looked at Charlie, who was standing behind Sterling. Since I had to look up at Charlie's face, the captain must have thought I found something real interesting on the wall behind him so he turned around and looked, too. There wasn't anything there but a yellowing map of Oak Valley with some plastic pushpins stuck in it here and there. Sterling turned back to me. "Well?" he said.

Well, what? *"What am I supposed to say, Charlie?"*
"Ask him to show you the dental records."
"Your dental records?"
"Who the hell else's dental records would I be talking about?"
"Don't snap at me, Charlie. I'm doing the best I can."
Charlie sighed. Jeez.

"May I see the dental records, Captain Sterling? Charlie Bilbo's dental records."

"What for?"

"I just want to."

"For chrissake. Hell, what difference does it make?"

Captain Sterling turned to his computer monitor which was on a leaf that jutted off the side of his desk. He hit a key and a cursor blipped on the screen. He typed in RI REQ: DENTAL RECORDS/BILBO, CHARLES J./ASAP/STERLING and hit the enter key.

"It's called a mail message, Charlie. He tells the computer what he wants and somebody else's computer beeps and even if they're using the computer for something else, they hit a button and the captain's message appears on their screen. Pretty neat, huh?"

"Uh-huh," Charlie said, but he didn't sound impressed. I'd already noticed that he wasn't surprised by all the changes since 1969. There are new buildings and people jogging with Walkmans on and, of course, the clothes are a lot different and so are the cars. Before we left the house I'd turned on the TV to the Weather Channel to be sure it wasn't going to rain— the weather's been nice but you can't always count on April not showering on you—and I told Charlie about cable TV and he just nodded like he already knew all about it and he wasn't even impressed with my big screen TV or the remote control. In the car, I'd listened to a CD and I know for sure they didn't have that kind of sound system in the 'sixties. Or that

kind of music. The CD was Pearl Jam's latest. I grew up listening to Duke and Lady's kind of music and Pearl Jam is pretty hot stuff compared to Simon and Garfunkle. Charlie tapped his fingers to the beat, but that was all.

I guess he'd kept tabs on how the world was progressing since his death. I guess that wouldn't be too bad. I always thought one of the bad things about dying was that you'd never know how things turned out. I used to get all weepy thinking that Duke and Lady died before I got the money, so they never got to see me living in a fancy house and wearing real diamond earrings. It's kind of nice to think that maybe they do know, that maybe they've been watching me. Although I sure hope Charlie wasn't lying about there being rules about how much you could see—like him not being able to watch me go to the bathroom—because I sure wouldn't want Duke and Lady peering over my shoulder while I was blowing some guy or something like that.

Captain Sterling seemed to be in a huffy mood all of a sudden. He was flipping through some papers on his desk and acting like I wasn't even there. I wondered if Charlie felt like that. But then he really wasn't there, was he? So maybe it didn't bother him. It made me feel a little antsy though, so I was glad when a woman cop came into the cubicle and handed Sterling a file folder. Sterling didn't even thank her so I tried to make up for it by smiling at her. She gave me a slow once-over, adding up price tags in her head, and left without a word. Sometimes life is easier when you make minimum wage plus tips.

Sterling handed me a dental x-ray. I held them up toward the light, like I really knew what I was looking for. Charlie stepped behind me, so I angled them to give him a good look.

"Those aren't my x-rays."

"Your name's on them, Charlie."

"They aren't mine. I have two fake teeth in a permanent bridge on the top left side."

"You do?"

"I beg your pardon?"

"Um ... What I meant was *do you* know much about these?"

"The x-rays? They're fairly simple. All the solid white sections are fillings." I lowered the x-ray and Captain Sterling pointed to three teeth with bright white on their surfaces. "Charlie had pretty good teeth. Only three fillings."

"He had two teeth missing on the top—"

"Left."

"—left side. He had a permanent bridge there."

"What?"

I told him one more time. He leaned back in his seat and looked at me like maybe I had two heads, or asparagus caught in my front teeth.

"How the hell would you know anything about Charlie Bilbo's teeth? Just what is your game, Ms. Lange?"

"It's not a game. These aren't Charlie Bilbo's dental x-rays. The bones in my backyard are Charlie Bilbo's. Did the skeleton have a permanent bridge on the top left side?"

"Way to go, Lizbet."

"I did not personally examine the remains. That's the medical examiner's job. These x-rays are Charlie Bilbo's. His name is on them. They've been in our files since he disappeared in nineteen sixty-nine. There was an explosion, Ms. Lange, and we had to identify three burned bodies. Two of them were cops. Charlie Bilbo's partners. The third one was a student activist named Samuel Towne. Bilbo didn't die in the explosion and he was never seen again. He disappeared and so did a million dollars. The consensus at the time—and still today—is that Charlie Bilbo grabbed the money, set off the explosive device, and is living off blood money to this day."

"Well, that just isn't true."

"Would you like to tell me exactly what did happen in nineteen sixty-nine, Ms. Lange? And after that you can explain how you know what happened before you were born."

I started searching through my handbag, like maybe I needed a Kleenex. *"Jeez, Charlie, what do I do now?"* Charlie said he didn't know. Big help. *"Listen, I know. Take the bottom paper from that stack on his desk and hold it up so I can see it and I'll tell him what it says—word for word, you know—and he'll be convinced I really am psychic."*

"I can't do that."

"What do you mean, you can't do it? Why not?"

"You wouldn't be able to read it. Like the art book, remember?"

"So you read it to me, I'll repeat it to him."

"I can't do that, either."

"Why not?"

"Because there could be no earthly explanation for your knowing what's on that paper."

"Earthly explanation. That's good, Charlie. Kind of a play on words, right? So don't read it to me, just read it yourself and give me a rough idea what it's about. It'll still impress the shit out of him."

"That would amount to the same thing. You'd know something you can't possibly know."

"Well, jeez, there's no earthly explanation for me knowing your name, either."

"That will be explained somehow. I don't know how, but it will. I can't interfere, Lizbet, I already explained that. I can't do things that could only be explained by the existence of paranormal abilities."

I'd rummaged around in my purse about as long as I could without Sterling deciding I was searching for my brains.

I pulled a tissue out, dabbed at my nose, then smiled at the captain. *"So what am I going to tell this guy, Charlie?"*

"Ask to see the skeleton."

"I'd like to see the skeleton."

"That isn't possible. I'm busy, Ms. Lange. I'd suggest you give some thought to explaining your connection to Charlie Bilbo. Otherwise ..." He gave me a cop look—real hard and threatening. It made me mad. I'm not a truck-stop waitress anymore.

"Otherwise what? You'll throw me in a cell and give me the third degree?"

Sterling smiled, not a very nice smile. "Otherwise, I don't feel like wasting my time with you." He stood up. "Goodbye, Ms. Lange. Give me a call if you change your mind."

Chapter Five

"So now what, Charlie?" We were back in the car, halfway up Foothill Avenue, which is the long winding road that leads up to the foothills, where all us rich people live. I've been living up there for three months and none of the neighbors have come by to introduce themselves. Even today, when all the commotion started and cop cars were parked all over the circular driveway in front of my house, I didn't see any of the neighbors rubbernecking. Sometimes I think I should just sell the house and move into a nice condo down on the south side of town, where the upper-middle-class people live. Or maybe I should move back to Gilroy. I fit in better there. Although I fit in best at the truck stop. At least I used to. I stopped going there a while back because it was just too awkward, me with all my money slumming with my old friends. They didn't treat me the same way anymore.

"We need to get a look at the bones."

"Don't you know if they're your bones?"

"Not really. I assume they are. They must be. Why else would I be here?"

"Well, old Captain Sterling won't let us look at them so you'll just have to think of something else."

"We have to see the bones. When we get back to the house, find

out where they are. The morgue used to be in the basement of St. Anthony's Hospital but I noticed it's been completely rebuilt."

"What makes you think Sterling will tell me?"

"Find out some other way."

"How?" But Charlie didn't answer. We drove the rest of the way to the house in silence. Well, not silence. I was playing an old Nirvana CD. The lead singer, Kurt Cobain, was twenty-seven when he died—another member of the Twenty-Seven Club.

All the great ones died young, Duke says. *Hendrix and Joplin, Jim Morrison, Harry Chapin. Patsy Cline and Jim Reeves—they were country singers, Lizzy.* He smokes for a while, then says, *Hell, maybe you're better off not being famous. All the best musicians seem to die young.* Duke and Lady look at each other when he says that. I don't understand the look, but somehow I know it has something to do with the old guitar in a cracked leather case in the hall closet that no one ever mentions. And then I look at Duke's left hand, at the three crooked fingers he can't bend because he got them caught in the machinery at the cannery when I was four years old.

Duke didn't know about Kurt Cobain joining the Twenty-Seven Club by killing himself because Duke died first, and he probably wouldn't have noticed anyway because he didn't really like any music after about 1970, which was the year Simon and Garfunkle split up. The Beatles split up in 1970, too. Lady told me that Duke was so upset he played all their albums over and over until she told him that if she had to listen to "Yellow Submarine" one more time she was going to take a hammer to his entire record collection.

Getting the information about the morgue turned out to be real easy. I called the police station and told the woman who answered that I was supposed to identify a body at the morgue but I didn't know where it was. She told me. I guess it's no big secret. It's in the basement of the new St. Anthony's hospital. She even gave me the phone number.

I called it, thinking maybe nobody would be there since it was after five o'clock and why would they guard the morgue? I mean, who would want to steal a body, or even look at one if they didn't have to? Maybe we could just walk right in and take a look at the bones. A guy answered the phone though.

"Um, hello," I said.

"What can I do you for?"

"Um ..." I looked at Charlie, who was staring at me with a very serious expression. He really wanted to see those bones. "My name's Li—Elizabeth Dutton. Captain John Sterling asked me to go down there—to the morgue—and take a look at the skeleton that was brought in today. I'm ... um, I'm a ... an expert on ... um, dentistry. When would be a convenient time?"

Charlie grinned and gave me a thumbs up gesture. I grinned back at him.

"Hey, come on down. It's so damn quiet down here I'm about to fall asleep. You know the way? You take the elevator to the basement, hang a right, follow the corridor to the end of the hall, make another right and then another right and it's the fourth door on the left. Can't miss it. Sign says AUTHORIZED PERSONNEL ONLY. Just knock and I'll let you in."

"Thank you. It'll take me about half an hour to get there."

"*No problema, señorita.* Ain't nothing kickin' down here but me and I'm stuck here all by my lonesome 'til midnight. See you when you get here. *Ciao.*"

I told Charlie what he'd said. "What if he checks with Sterling?"

"*Why would he? He seems to have bought your story. He's just a morgue attendant. A babysitter, more or less. Why should he care who comes down to look at a body? Let's go.*"

Thirty-five minutes later we were walking down a corridor in the basement of St. Anthony's. It was brightly lit but completely empty. We didn't run into a single soul. Although it occurred to me that there might be some down there that I couldn't see.

We'd made the first right turn when I said, "Listen, Charlie, why don't you just go in there yourself and take a look at the bones? Nobody'll know you're there. You can move the bones around and everything. Jeez, you can twirl your armbone like a baton and no one'll see you. You don't really need me."

"What good would that do? I already told you I can't tell you things you don't have any way to know. If I can't tell you what I find out, what good is it? Besides, I can't go in there without you."

"Why not?"

"I guess I didn't explain it very well."

"Explain what?"

"You're my link."

"Link? What's that mean?"

"I told you to think of it as parallel universes, right? Well, to get from one to the other I have to establish some kind of link between the two universes. You're my link. I can't just go wandering around without you."

"You mean you have to stay close to me? Or what happens?"

"I lose contact with your universe."

"What would happen if you lost contact? Something bad?"

"No, nothing bad. I could make contact with you again. But I can't leave you and do things on my own. I can't stay in your universe if the link is broken."

"So just exactly how close to me do you have to be?"

"Fairly close."

"But you disappeared once, out in the backyard when I was talking to the FBI guys."

"I disappeared from your sight. You didn't disappear from mine. I was there, I just didn't let you see me."

"That is *so* creepy, Charlie. Okay, how about this: You open the door, like you did the bathroom door this morning. I'll be able to see into the room and you can show me the bones."

"That won't work. You wouldn't be able to see inside the room."

"I saw you when you went out of the bathroom. You were standing in the hall waiting for me."

Charlie shook his head. *"You don't really think you can see through a closed door, do you? You already know what your hallway looks like. Your mind was just filling in the blanks. You don't know what the morgue looks like so if I go into it, I'll just disappear. You have to go in, Lizbet."*

I sighed a few times, but Charlie didn't seem to notice. We came to the door with the AUTHORIZED PERSONNEL ONLY sign. I tapped on it and it swung open.

The man who opened the door was short but broad and his face reminded me a little of Jeff Bridges in *Starman*. He looked a little spacey, too. He looked me up and down slowly and said, "Hey, hey, hey. Step into my parlor." He moved back and bowed. I giggled. He was the kind of guy I was used to. Not like my lawyer and my financial manager and my stock broker and all the other horribly *dignified* men I've had to deal with since Tom died.

I walked into the morgue. Just the word's enough to make you gag, but it wasn't really that bad. It was a big room with banks of drawers built into one wall and some cold-looking steel tables in the middle. One of them had a white sheet draped over it but whatever was beneath the sheet wasn't big enough to be a body. Then I realized Charlie's bones must be on that table and I shivered.

"My name's Pete. You need anything, and I mean anything, you just let me know. Got your man right over here. He's all put together. The doc said it was like putting together a jigsaw puzzle. He kinda fell apart when the 'dozer dug him up."

He carefully lifted the sheet off. And there were Charlie's bones. I'd only glanced at them that morning when the Splash 'N Shine guy came and got me. All the dirt had been cleaned off since then. They weren't as white as I'd expected, but otherwise they looked about the way you'd expect a skeleton to look. The bones weren't hooked together, just lying in the right places. It really wasn't any spookier than a Halloween decoration. As long as I didn't think about them being a real person's bones.

Down by the feet, there were some other things that I couldn't figure out at first. Then I realized they were what was left of Charlie's leather vest and sandals and belt. I guess everything else rotted away.

I leaned over to take a good look at the jaw. Charlie had told me to bring a notebook so I'd look official, so I opened it up and got out a pen.

"You missed Sterling by about fifteen minutes," Pete said.

I jumped a little and straightened up to look at him. "I did? Um, did you tell him I was coming?"

"Nah. Me 'n Sterling don't hit it off real good. I don't give 'im the time of day if I can help it. He's always popping in here wanting something done yesterday. He was pretty pissed about your man here though."

"Oh? Why?"

"Shit, I dunno. Something about the teeth. He said, 'Sonofabitch'—excuse my French—'that's a goddamn bridge.' Musta thought they'd identified Mr. Bones here and the bridge screwed it up, huh? That's your whaddayacallit, area of expertise, right? Sterling shoulda waited 'til you checked it out. Sonofabitch is always wanting everything yesterday."

"Well," I said, "I'll be sure he gets my report first thing tomorrow." I turned back to the skeleton. Charlie was standing on the other side of the table. He pointed at the left upper jaw. The bridge wasn't in good shape. It was hanging down because one end had broken off, but even I could tell that it was a bridge with two fake teeth. *"It really is you ... um, yours, isn't it, Charlie?"*

"Definitely. Somebody switched the dental x-rays twenty-seven years ago, assuming Sterling was telling the truth. That means ..."

"What?"

"A cover-up of some kind. It had to be someone in the department. Who else could have switched the x-rays?"

"The dentist?"

"I don't think so. I went to the same dentist ever since I was a kid. James McMillan. He'd be old now, seventy-five or eighty, if he's still alive. I don't think he could have been involved. He was just a dentist. Somebody had to switch the x-rays after he sent them to the police department and that means it had to be someone in the department."

While we talked, I'd been scribbling numbers and making little sketches in my notebook. I closed it and smiled at Pete. "You've been very helpful. I really appreciate it."

"No problema. You got everything you need? You want a copy of the x-rays? Nice thing about dead people is you don't have to worry about overdosing them with radiation so we take extra x-rays of the teeth so when some agency, like another police department somewhere, wants a copy, we already got one handy."

"Why, thank you. Yes, I think I'd like a copy of them."

He went to a file cabinet and brought back a large manila folder. I glanced inside at the x-rays and thanked him again.

"Anything else, Charlie?"

"Not that I can think of. I'm impressed, Lizbet. I couldn't have done it better myself."

I smiled and I guess it must have been a really good smile because Pete thought it was for him and asked if we could get together sometime. He was pretty persistent but I managed to get to the door and tell him goodbye without making him mad.

"Come back anytime," he said. "Anytime at all. *Adios, amiga. Ciao.*"

We went back to the elevator and took it up to the main floor. On our way out we passed the security office, which had a big window so the security people could watch the lobby. As I glanced in, a man tapped another one on the shoulder and they both turned around and stared at me. There were at least a dozen video monitors in there, showing different parts of the hospital, entrances mostly, and hallways. One screen showed a long empty corridor. Like the long empty corridor in the basement. Where I'd just been. Where I'd talked to Charlie. They must have watched me walking down an empty corridor talking to myself. I felt my face turning red and I couldn't get out of there fast enough. I'm surprised Charlie managed to keep up with me.

Chapter Six

We went home and I ordered a pizza and ate it in the family room. Charlie had some pizza, too. We didn't talk much. Later on, I turned the television on and sat through a bunch of sitcoms. It was kind of a relief not having to talk to Charlie, if you really want to know. At ten, I flipped channels to a local news program. The discovery of the skeleton in my backyard was mentioned, but no one seemed real excited about it. Next, there was an interview with the chief of police of Oak Valley. He was on television all the time, yakking about the crime rate or the police department budget or what a good job he was doing. I never liked watching him. He had a very intense stare that made me feel like he knew everything I'd ever done wrong. I turned the television off.

"Charlie? Why were you in my backyard?"

"I wasn't. I didn't die here. It happened in an abandoned warehouse on the north side of town. Whoever shot me brought my body up here to dispose of it."

"Maybe we should find out who owned the house then."

"Good idea."

"My lawyer should be able to tell me, don't you think?"

"Sure. You can call him in the morning."

"Okay. Was it a drug thing you were working on?"

"No. I had infiltrated SAMIC."

"Sammick? What's that?"

"It's an acronym. S-A-M-I-C. Students Against the Military-Industrial Complex. There were a lot of activist groups back then, protesting the war in Vietnam. A lot of them were harmless, just a bunch of kids carrying signs and making noise. SAMIC was started by some students at Oak Valley College and at first it was just another student protest group, then it was taken over by a man named Samuel Towne. He was a real radical. Advocated the violent overthrow of the government, stuff like that."

"He was one of the bodies they identified after the explosion. That's what Sterling said."

"Yeah. Under Towne's leadership, SAMIC became really radical. We thought they were responsible for a couple of bank bombings, but we didn't have any proof. That's why I went undercover and joined the group: We were trying to get some evidence on the bombings. I'd been with SAMIC for almost three months and Towne trusted me. The more I found out about the group, the scarier it got. Towne had contacts with organized crime and that was bad enough, but he also linked up with an international terrorist organization that wanted to use SAMIC for its own purposes.

"Towne needed money, so he made a deal with the terrorists. SAMIC was going to kidnap a prominent politician who was scheduled to deliver the graduation speech at Oak Valley College on the tenth of June. They were going to hold him for ransom, only they weren't going to ask for money. They were supposed to demand the release of some political prisoners. That's what the terrorist group wanted. In exchange, they'd give SAMIC a million dollars, which Towne wanted to use to buy assault weapons, among other things. I never did find out what country was backing the terrorists, but they weren't hurting for money.

"You know that old saying, there's no honor among thieves? It's

true. Towne didn't trust the terrorists so he insisted on getting the cash up front. The terrorists didn't trust him so they agreed to give it to him only if it was placed in a safe at the SAMIC headquarters and the terrorists were allowed to guard it round the clock until after the kidnapping. SAMIC's headquarters was the abandoned warehouse where I was killed. Towne trusted me, like I said, so he assigned me to be one of the guards guarding the terrorist guards who were guarding the safe. I set up a bust. I had enough evidence by then to connect them with the bombings, so we figured we could put them out of action. We needed to make our move before the tenth so the politician would be out of danger. It was set up for the night of the eighth of June, two-thirty in the morning. June ninth, actually.

"Something went wrong. Towne came down to the warehouse about midnight, two hours before he was due to relieve me. He was real nervous, I could tell that, and he kept looking at me. I asked him what was wrong and he called me a pig. Slang for a cop back then."

"Still is."

"I knew I was in big trouble. The terrorist guards didn't speak much English so I don't think they had any idea Towne was mad at me. He couldn't let them know he'd found out I was a cop. They'd realize SAMIC was under surveillance and they'd pull out of the deal and Towne wanted that money bad. He pulled a gun on me, making sure the terrorists didn't see it. He took me into another room and tied me up in a chair with my back to the door. I couldn't see my watch but it seemed like a long time passed. Then I heard someone open the door and walk up behind me and I heard the sound of a gun being cocked and that was the end of me. Whoever shot me got my body out of there before the bomb went off and he must be the one who got away with the money. The safe would have survived an explosion. It must have been emptied out."

"Why would he move your body? Why not just let you be blown up with rest of them?"

Charlie smiled. *"Wild guess? He wanted a patsy. With me missing, and presumably still alive, I was the perfect suspect."*

"And they fell for it. The cops think you took the money and you've been hiding out ever since. They think you blew the building up, too, and killed those two cops and Samuel Towne."

"And someone switched the dental x-rays so even if my body was found, it wouldn't be identified."

"Well, if they'd found it right away, they'd know it was you. I mean, you'd still look like yourself."

"I'm sure he took care of that. Got rid of my fingerprints and face with acid or—"

"Yuk, Charlie."

"Sorry. Anyway, if they found a body that had been ... um ... mutilated, they'd use the teeth for identification and with the switched dental records they'd never connect the body with me or the explosion or SAMIC. That's probably why he came all the way up here to get rid of my body, to make sure no one suspected there was a connection if it was found. You're right, we need to find out who owned the house then. This isn't the kind of neighborhood you just wander around in until you find a good place to bury a body."

"First thing in the morning, okay? I'm kinda tired, Charlie. It's been a long day. I'm going to bed."

We went upstairs to my bedroom, which isn't a single room. It's a suite. A bedroom, a bathroom, a dressing room, a sitting room, a closet that's about the size of my old studio apartment. Plus a balcony with a stairway leading down to the patio. There's a Jacuzzi in the bathroom. And a bidet. And enough floor space to dance the Achy-Breaky.

I went into the dressing room and closed the door behind me, hoping Charlie would get the message. I changed into a nightgown and robe, then went into the bathroom, which has a door connecting it to the dressing room. When

I finished in there, I went back into the bedroom and sat on the edge of the bed.

Charlie was standing at the foot of the bed. "How come you know some things that happened after you died but not others? I mean, you know your wife divorced you and moved away but you don't know for sure who shot you."

He shrugged. *"I just know about that. I don't know why. That's the only thing I know. I don't make the rules."*

I started to ask who did, but I changed my mind. He'd probably tell me it was classified information and, besides, I wasn't all that sure I really wanted to know.

"Are you just going to stand there all night?"

"What do you want me to do?"

"I don't know. At least sit down."

He sat on the window seat. I turned off the light and took off my robe and got under the covers. God, I was so tired. But my eyes wouldn't stay closed and all kinds of thoughts kept jumbling through my mind. I rolled over a few times and kept turning the pillow over to the cool side. I knew a sure-fire way to make myself relax enough to go to sleep. But not with Charlie in the room.

I jumped a little when Charlie spoke, his voice quiet. *"Would you like me to leave, Lizbet? Can you sleep better if I'm not here?"*

I sat up and peered at him. He even looked ghostly then, backlit by moonlight streaming through the sheer curtains. He looked perfectly innocent, not smirky or anything. I decided maybe he hadn't been reading my mind.

"Actually, I think I could. Sleep better if you weren't here, I mean."

"I'll see you in the morning." And he was gone, just like that.

I lay back down again, wondering if he was really gone or if I just couldn't see him anymore. I finally decided it didn't really matter. It wasn't like he could *tell* anyone. I closed my eyes and worked on a fantasy. I kind of have the hots for my stockbroker, who's real cute even if he is a stuffy fuddy-duddy, and he doesn't have to be a fuddy-duddy in my fantasies so I tried to think of him but Charlie's face kept getting in the way. So in the end, it was Charlie in my fantasy, and he worked real good.

I slept like a log, except that I woke up once, sometime in the middle of the night. I'd had a strange dream: I was back in the morgue and I was picking up the things at the foot of Charlie's skeleton and I was holding them up and naming them: *Charlie's vest, Charlie's sandal, Charlie's other sandal, Charlie's belt.* In my dream, it seemed really important to name each one, but once I was awake it didn't make any sense at all, so I just turned the pillow over to the cool side again and went back to sleep.

Chapter Seven

Charlie wasn't there—at least he wasn't visible—when I got up in the morning, so I put on a leotard and ran downstairs to the rec room and did twenty minutes on the stationary bike and ten minutes on the stairstepper, then I ran back upstairs and soaked in the tub and washed and dried my hair and spent a few minutes in the closet picking out something to wear. White pants and a pale blue cotton-knit sweater with short puffy sleeves and real pretty hand-crocheted trim. White sandals. I dumped all the junk from my peach purse into a white one in case I had to go somewhere in a hurry. When I was putting the peach purse on a closet shelf I noticed the box of Duke and Lady's hippie stuff.

I opened it up and pulled out a peace symbol on a chain. I have pictures of Lady and Duke wearing it. Not at the same time; they shared it. I used to play with it when I was a kid. It was bright and shiny then, but it isn't real silver so now it's discolored, sort of a rusty brown. I thought about showing it to Charlie, thinking maybe he'd be interested in old hippie stuff but I just put it back in the box instead. Charlie's peace symbol was real silver and turquoise. It wouldn't get all old and ugly-looking like Duke and Lady's.

1969. The Year of Woodstock. Lots of other things happened that year, too. That was the year Mary Jo Kopechne drowned when Teddy Kennedy drove his car off a bridge on Chappaquiddick Island in Massachusetts. Duke always said we would have had a second President Kennedy, if the senator hadn't left the scene of the accident, because he was sure to be nominated by the Democrats in 1972 and Duke figured everyone would be so sick of Nixon by then that even the Republicans would vote for Kennedy. But Kennedy didn't run and Nixon was re-elected and then there was all that Watergate stuff later on.

Duke and Lady went to Woodstock in '69. Some astronauts went a little farther—all the way to the moon. *The eagle has landed,* Duke says between tokes. *That's what they said: "Houston, Tranquillity Base here. The Eagle has landed." The Eagle was their lunar module, Lizzy-Liz, kind of a mini-spaceship Neil Armstrong and Buzz Aldrin used to get from the big Apollo 11 spaceship to the moon. The other astronauts stayed in the Apollo 11, orbiting the moon while Neil Armstrong took his small step for a man and a giant leap for mankind.*

Womankind didn't count for much back then, Lady says. *But we were working on it.*

As I slid the box of memorabilia back onto the closet shelf, I suddenly had a strange feeling, like *déjà vu* only it wasn't like this same thing had happened before, it was more like I had a thought that I couldn't quite get hold of. Then the feeling went away. I shrugged and closed the closet door.

Tingle.

"Hi, Charlie."

"Good morning. Did you sleep well?"

"Mm-hm. How about you?"

He laughed. I guess because he doesn't have to sleep.

"Let me get something to eat and then I'll call my lawyer

and find out who owned the house in nineteen sixty-nine, okay?"

My lawyer's name is Fernando DeSilva. I kind of inherited him from Tom. It turned out he was in court and it was after ten when he finally called me back. I told him what I wanted to know and he didn't even have to look anything up. The people Tom bought the house from were the original owners.

"It was built in the late 'sixties, Lizbet. 'Sixty-eight? Somewhere around there. Mr. and Mrs. Altman lived in it until sometime in the 'eighties—'eighty-seven, I think—then they moved to a smaller house and their son and his wife moved in. The Altmans still owned it though and they put it on the market when their son got divorced and moved to L.A. last year. Tom had already been looking for something in that area so he snapped it right up. You must know Mr. and Mrs. Altman."

I must? "Um, no, I don't know them."

"No? They live right down the street from you. That small gray stone house with the lions by the gate."

Small gray stone house? It had to have fifteen rooms. Of course, mine has more so I guess Altman's house qualifies as small. *Smaller* at least.

"I've never met them. I guess I'm not very neighborly."

DeSilva chuckled. "They'd love you, my dear. Introduce yourself sometime."

I said I would and thanked him for the information.

And wouldn't you know as soon as I told Charlie, he came up with this bright idea that I should go introduce myself to the Altmans. Like right this minute.

I wanted to call them first, but naturally their number was unlisted so we got in the Porsche and drove to their house. All the houses up here are on huge lots so "right down the street" is about a mile and a half.

The door was opened by a maid. In a uniform. That's how I knew she was the maid, not Mrs. Altman. Also because she was black and I was pretty sure no black people bought a house up here in the 'sixties. They were still trying to get to the front of the bus back then. I know all about it because Duke and Lady saw Martin Luther King, Jr., in 1965 in Selma, Alabama, where he was leading civil rights demonstrators on a 50-mile walk from Selma to the state capitol in Montgomery. I only heard the story about a zillion times. Duke and Lady were just kids and they hitchhiked clear across the country to Alabama. Their parents were really pissed when they finally showed up at home again.

I told the maid who I was and she led me and Charlie to a room she called the parlor. Of course, she didn't know Charlie was with me. She said she'd let Mrs. Altman know I was there and she went away.

The parlor was full of that dark wood furniture with curvy legs—Queen Anne, I think—and the upholstery was dark green and gold and so was the wallpaper. I sat down in a chair by the fireplace and crossed my legs at the ankle and clasped my hands in my lap. Little Miss Priss. I had butterflies in my stomach. Rich people scare me.

I heard someone coming a few minutes later and I jumped up like maybe I expected to be yelled at for sitting on the furniture. Mrs. Altman didn't look anything like I expected. For one thing, I thought all rich women were skinny and Mrs. Altman definitely wasn't. She was short and round and gray-haired and looked like somebody's grandmother. She was wearing black slacks and a black-and-white blouse and had a long string of pearls around her neck.

"How nice of you to come visit, Lizbet. May I call you Lizbet? Would you care for some tea? Margo—the cook, dear—

made some lovely pastries this morning. Shall I have her bring us some? Oh, sit down, dear. Please, make yourself right at home. We don't stand on ceremony around here. Walter— that's Mr. Altman—Walter and I are just two old homebodies. Walter's always wandering around in the yard in a horribly baggy old sweatsuit that's just his absolute favorite outfit and I'm always saying, Walter, what on earth will the neighbors think? But I'm just joking, of course. My goodness, let the man be comfortable is what I always say. He isn't here, I'm afraid. He had to go into the City this week to attend to some business. Let me just ring the kitchen and ask Margo to send us some tea and we'll sit down and have a nice chat."

I don't know about Mrs. Altman, but I was out of breath just listening to her. I sat down again in the same chair. She spoke into the phone briefly, then sat down in a matching chair angled toward mine.

"Now, Lizbet," she said. "Tell me all about yourself. Such a tragedy, your dear husband passing away so suddenly. My goodness, we hadn't even had a chance to send an invitation to one of our little dinner parties when he passed on. Of course, we were abroad when he first moved in—you were away, too, weren't you, dear? I don't remember anyone mentioning you—and then right after we came home we heard the sad news. Such a tragedy. Still there was quite an age difference, wasn't there? So I suppose it was something you had steeled yourself for. But I suppose even so ..."

She trailed off as the maid came into the room with a tray and set it on the table between us. I decided not to try to explain about me and Tom being divorced. It was too complicated. Besides, I didn't think I'd ever get the chance. Charlie was standing behind me so I couldn't see his reaction to Mrs. Altman. Probably just as well. I would have got the giggles.

"Now, where were we? Thank you, Mimi. That will be all." Mimi nodded and left. "Oh, yes, your poor husband. Well, Lizbet—you don't mind if I call you Lizbet, do you? Such a charming name. I really think you're wise not to spend too much time in mourning. My goodness, it's been what? Three months at least? Of course, women used to positively bury themselves in black for *years,* but how foolish. Life must go on. That's what I always say to Walter, life must go on. Why, I told him just the other day that I don't intend to—I'm sorry, dear, what is it?"

Whew! She'd finally noticed that I was trying to get a word in edgewise. "I was wondering if I could ask you some questions about my house."

"Well, of course, dear." She poured a cup of tea and handed it to me, talking all the time. "We had it custom-made, you know. Charles Gorsham was the architect. He's dead now, of course, but he did all the best houses back then. Quite an interesting man. Gay, you know, but in those days no one really mentioned things like that. What was that, dear?"

I'd figured out that the only way to stop her was to go ahead and talk while she was. If you waited for her to pause, you'd wait all day. I repeated my question. "When was it built? What year?"

"Oh, it was quite a disaster at the time. My goodness, I thought Walter was going to have a stroke. It was supposed to be finished in January but, well, you know how it goes, there was one delay after another and it was summer before we could move in."

"What year?"

"Why, nineteen sixty-nine. It was Walter's gift to me for our tenth anniversary."

"When did you move in? In the summer, but what month?"

"Why, in June. June tenth, I always remember the date because it was exactly five months after our anniversary and I said to Walter, Walter, it's exactly five months late but I love it anyway."

"Hear that, Charlie? No one was living there when you died."

"I heard. Ask her about the yard."

"The yard? Oh, I get it."

Mrs. Altman had been going on and on about how the tenth anniversary is the Tin Anniversary—like the twenty-fifth being the Silver Anniversary, you know—but who on earth wants something made out of tin, is what she had thought, but Walter had the most adorable bracelet designed for her, made of tin, of course, and gave it to her on their anniversary since the house wasn't finished.

I jumped in. "Was the lawn already in when you moved in? The back lawn?"

Mrs. Altman leaned back in her chair and didn't say anything for at least thirty seconds. I took a drink of my tea and picked up one of the pastries and bit into it. Real flaky pastry with apricots. I wondered if maybe I could hire Margo away from her.

"Oh, my dear," Mrs. Altman said. "You're here about that horrible skeleton, aren't you? The police have already talked to us, you know that, don't you? I'll tell you exactly what I told them: Walter and I did not bury a body in our backyard. Why, the very idea is preposterous. Not that the police accused us, of course. Obviously the body had been there before the house was built. It was all woods then, you know. Quite a few trees had to be felled to make room for the house. Although, it's still a very pretty lot. I do like a lot of trees, don't you?"

"Yeah. I mean, yes. I was just wondering when the lawn was put in. To narrow down the time, you know. I mean, he—

the body—must have been buried before your lawn was put in. You would have noticed if someone dug up your lawn."

"Why, certainly we would have. It was the very last thing. We could have moved in earlier, but Walter wanted everything perfect. I hadn't even seen the house, you know. It was a big surprise. Oh, I knew he was having one built, but I didn't know where exactly and I'd never seen it."

"Exactly when—"

"The lawn? Why, it was just the day before we moved in. June ninth, that would have been. They had been working on it for quite some time. Leveling the ground and tilling it all up to prepare it for the sod. They used sod, those strips of grass they unroll and just like that you have a lovely yard. Walter would have preferred to have the lawn seeded—he said it makes a healthier lawn—but the whole thing had already dragged on for so long, he had them do it that way so it would be done quickly and it would look just perfect when I finally saw it and we never had a bit of trouble with that lawn, not a bit."

"On June ninth the backyard would have been nice soft dirt, tilled up and ready for planting. Perfect for burying a body. All he had to do was smooth out the surface afterward and no one would ever know a grave had been dug there."

"Yeah, Charlie. Is there anything else I should ask her?"

"I can't think of anything. See if you can cut it short and let's get out of here."

"Do you remember the name of the landscape company, Mrs. Altman?"

"Good idea, Lizbet."

"Why, Braverman's, of course. They're the best. The sons are running it now, of course, but they're still the only place to go. Oh, of course, you'll be needing some landscaping once your pool is in, won't you? Oh, do call Braverman's. They really are the best."

I ate two more pastries before Mrs. Altman ever stopped talking long enough for me to say I needed to leave. She walked me to the door herself, although Mimi was there and opened it for me. Mimi winked at me. She knew a truck-stop waitress when she saw one.

We were at the end of the long driveway and turning onto the road before either of us said anything. "Well, she was really very nice, wasn't she?"

"Yeah, she was. Nice."

I made the mistake of looking at Charlie and he burst out laughing and I started giggling and we laughed and giggled all the way home.

Chapter Eight

I stopped laughing in a hurry when I turned into my driveway. There was an unmarked police car parked by the house, but it had been there all day because a couple cops were sifting through the dirt in the backyard. Now a dark sedan was parked behind it. And Captain John Sterling was standing on the porch.

It's pretty hard to miss a bright red Porsche so I figured he'd already seen me and there wasn't much point in backing out of the driveway in a hurry. I parked behind his car and got out.

Charlie said, *"At least he's still on the case."*

Like I was really worried about that. *"For god's sake, Charlie, he's probably going to arrest me for impersonating a dentist at the morgue."*

Charlie laughed. Why not? Nobody was going to slap handcuffs on *him* and drag him off to jail.

Sterling nodded hello and said he needed to talk to me. We went in the house and I led him to the formal living room, which is done in cream and pale blue. I sat on the couch and he sat in an armchair near it.

I smiled brightly and asked what he wanted.

"I spent the morning trying to track down a dentist named

James McMillan. Charlie Bilbo's dentist, the one we got the x-rays from."

"Uh-huh."

"James McMillan is dead, died about ten years ago. He was still working when he died so all his records were sent to other dentists, whoever his patients wanted to see after he died."

"Uh-huh."

"Those were his active cases, people he was still seeing. The patients he hadn't seen in years, like Charlie Bilbo, those records weren't sent to other dentists. Don't know where they are yet but there's a woman—a Mrs. Yakamoto—who worked in his office who might know. I haven't been able to get hold of her yet."

"Uh-huh. So you're trying to find Charlie's records. That's a good idea."

Sterling had this kind of bemused look on his face. I didn't understand it at first, then I realized he probably thought it was a little strange that I'd refer to a man I claimed had died before I was born by his first name, like he was a friend or something.

"Could be someone in McMillan's office dumped all the old files after he died. I won't know 'til I talk to this Mrs. Yakamoto. The reason I'm trying to track down the records—"

"—is because the skeleton has two fake teeth in a permanent bridge on the top left side."

Sterling leaned back in the chair and sighed and brushed some dandruff of the front of his suit jacket and said, "Pete Coogan's been given strict orders never to let anyone in the morgue again without the proper authorization. But you knew about the bridge before you went down there. How, Ms. Lange?"

"Um ..."

"And don't give me any of that 'I'm psychic' crap, either."

"I saw the skeleton when it was in the backyard."

"And you noticed the bridge? That's a little hard to believe. I was there, lady. If I remember correctly you didn't want to get anywhere near a bunch of bones."

"Don't call me *lady.*"

"Sorry. A bad habit. I didn't mean any disrespect. Used to be ... women didn't mind so much."

It wasn't that. Jeez, the truckers used to call me sweetie and honey and it never bothered me, as long as they didn't stiff me on the tip. I just didn't want to be called *lady.* It was my mother's name. "That's all right," I said. "You can call me Lizbet if you want."

"Lizbet. Okay. Look, I can tell you don't trust me. That's okay, I can understand that, but if you're mixed up with Charlie Bilbo you're biting off more than you can chew. You seem like a real nice gir—I mean, woman, and I wouldn't want you to go getting yourself into something you can't handle. So how about telling me what you know about Bilbo."

I didn't answer him. I asked Charlie what I should do and he shrugged. Real big help.

Sterling sighed. "Let me tell you what I'm doing. I got a skeleton I'm trying to identify. No big deal. Bodies turn up all the time. We either identify them or we don't. Something happened twenty-five, thirty years ago, what's the big deal? Probably whoever put the stiff in the ground's already kicked the bucket, right? So I was just going through the routine when the FBI tells me you say the skeleton's Charlie Bilbo. Charlie Bilbo. That's like saying it's Hitler, or Judas."

I glanced at Charlie but he was just standing there watching Sterling and didn't look mad or anything. Maybe ghosts don't get their feelings hurt.

"Did you know Charlie?"

"No, I was just a rookie patrolman. Started about three months before Bilbo disappeared. He was working undercover. Far as I know, I never saw him. I remember the night he disappeared, though. Never forget it. Not a cop on the force'll ever forget it."

"What happened?"

He grinned at me. "Your psychic powers on the blink? Just joking. Okay, it was all in the papers, anyway. No big secret. It was June eighth, nineteen sixty-nine. June ninth really since it was two-thirty in the morning. There was a big bust supposed to go down. A bunch of radicals and terrorists were holed up in an old warehouse out on the north end of town. Bilbo was undercover, like I said. He'd infiltrated the organization and set up the bust. Supposed to be a million dollars in a safe in the building, plus the ringleader, guy named Samuel Towne, and some foreign terrorists.

"Bilbo was supposed to leave the building at two o'clock and drive off. The SWAT team was supposed to get into position, then at two-thirty Bilbo was going to come back on foot and get the guys inside the building to open the door, big door like a garage door but reinforced steel. It was the only way to get into the building, except for a second-floor door you had to climb a fire escape to get to. All the other doors and the windows were sealed off. Bilbo was supposed to say his car broke down so he had to come back. They trusted him, thought he was one of them, you know, so they'd open the door for him and when they did the SWAT team was going to storm the place."

"What happened?"

"He never came back. There were some lookouts stationed outside the building. They saw him leave right on schedule. Two o'clock just like clockwork that door opened and Bilbo drove out in his VW bug and headed down the street. Never came back, though. Reason they wanted to do it that way, have him leave and then come back, was because he was supposed to call in to verify Samuel Towne was there and also to let the SWAT team know how many other guys were in the building, what they were armed with, stuff like that. He never called. Never came back. So, two-thirty in the morning the SWAT team's sitting out there wondering what the hell went wrong, when all of a sudden the door opens. So the SWAT team decides what the hell, the door's open, let's do it. The first two guys get through the door and one of them runs into a trip wire and *BOOM!* the whole building goes up."

"I was right, Lizbet. Someone in the police department was behind the whole thing. No one else would have known when the SWAT team was going to make its move."

I nodded. "Only three bodies were found, Samuel Towne and the two cops. There should have been more, right?"

"Yeah, Bilbo set it up for that night because Towne was supposed to relieve him—he was on guard duty and Towne was supposed to get there before two o'clock. There also should've been a couple other guys there, some terrorists who were guarding the money. See, the terrorists paid Towne to pull off a kidnapping and they didn't trust him not to double-cross them so they were guarding the money until the kidnapping was over."

"But how did all those other men get out of the building if there were cops outside?"

Sterling shrugged. "Left before one-thirty, most likely. SWAT team didn't get there 'til then. Didn't see any reason to have lookouts any earlier than that, what with Bilbo inside. Anything unusual happened, he would've told them about it when he called in his report."

"So what everyone thinks is that Charlie got rid of the guards somehow—"

"Probably told them he was a cop and let them leave, maybe even gave them some of the money. Who knows? They were all just a bunch of mercenaries. Probably glad to get out with their asses intact."

"And then Charlie rigged a bomb and took the money and at two o'clock he drove off and disappeared."

"Yep, that's it. The third body was identified as Samuel Towne."

"And everyone thinks it was all Charlie's doing."

"It had to be. No one else knew when the SWAT team was planning to make its move. The money was gone and Bilbo hasn't been seen since. Which brings us back to why I'm here. What the hell makes you think that skeleton is Charlie Bilbo?"

I didn't answer. What was I supposed to say? That I knew they were Charlie's bones because Charlie told me so? Sterling didn't say anything, either. After a couple minutes, he sighed and heaved himself up out of the chair. "I'll be seeing you again, Ms. Lange."

"Wait. You must believe me. Or at least you must wonder if I'm right. That's why you're trying to find the dental records, isn't it?"

"No, that isn't why. I don't think those bones are Bilbo's. I think the sonofabitch took the money and ran, sold out his fellow cops for cold hard cash. Reason I want to find McMillan's old records isn't so I can see if the skeleton is Bilbo's. You see, Ms. Lange, you gave me an idea when you said those x-rays weren't Bilbo's. I started thinking about how Samuel Towne's body was identified through dental records. Wasn't much of him left after the explosion. And I started thinking what if that wasn't really Towne's body? What if Charlie Bilbo and

Samuel Towne were in it together? Makes sense to me. From what I've heard about Towne he was too slick an operator to let Bilbo get the jump on him. And I started thinking maybe Towne wanted to disappear and he got the dentist to switch his records or maybe he managed to switch them himself. So what I did is, I pulled Towne's file, thinking I'd see if I could authenticate the records somehow. And guess what?"

"We went to the same dentist."

"He went to the same dentist as Charlie."

"Bingo, Ms. Lange. Not too surprising. Oak Valley was a lot smaller in nineteen sixty-nine. Weren't more than half a dozen dentists in the whole town."

"I recommended McMillan to Towne. He had a tooth bothering him and I gave him my dentist's name."

"So you aren't looking for Charlie's records, you're looking for Towne's."

"You got it. The way I see it is, if I can prove that wasn't Towne's body, I'll be sitting pretty come September when the promotion board meets."

"Jeez. That's pretty ... That's all you're interested in? Getting promoted?"

"What's wrong with that? I think Bilbo's still alive and I'm starting to think Towne is, too. I don't know what your angle is, but I'm going to find out. And when I do, well, Ms. Lange, you keep bad company you're gonna get burned. I'll be going now. You think it over and when you come to your senses, give me a call."

I followed him to the door and watched him drive off. Charlie was with me, naturally. It was like being Siamese twins or something. "What am I going to do, Charlie? He thinks I'm mixed up with you *and* Samuel Towne now."

"Relax. The only reason he told you what he's doing is to throw

a scare into you. He's doing this on his own, Lizbet. He can't even take you in for questioning without involving other people in the department and he's not going to do it because he wants all the glory for himself. He knows you aren't going to run to some other cop with a crazy story about knowing whose bones they are. There's nothing to worry about. I'm dead and Towne's dead, so how's he going to come up with evidence connecting you to either of us?"

"Are you sure Towne's dead? What if he's right, what if Towne's x-rays were switched, too? We know for a fact yours were."

"If Towne didn't die in nineteen sixty-nine, he's up to no good somewhere. He wasn't kidding around, Lizbet. He was a madman. Power was the only thing that mattered to him. If he's alive, he's sure to be mixed up with some subversive organization somewhere. It seems to me the Feds would have found out he was still around, even if they couldn't manage to pin anything on him. It's hard to believe he could keep such a low profile that no one would identify him in twenty-seven years. Sterling's probably going to be tailing you."

"What? You mean *following* me?"

"Sure. Why do you think he told you about the dental records? He's hoping you'll either lead him straight to me, or Towne, or else one of us will try to get the dental records before he does and destroy them. He even told you the name of the woman who worked for McMillan—twice, in fact. Mrs. Yakamoto. How many Yakamotos do you suppose there are in the phone book?"

"*Following* me! Oh, *god*, Charlie. What have you gotten me into?"

Chapter Nine

There were eight Yakamotos in the phone book. I only looked because I was curious. Charlie said it didn't make any sense for us to chase after the dental records when Captain Sterling was going to do it for us.

"But what about your dental records, Charlie? We need to prove the skeleton's yours, don't we?"

"Trust me, Lizbet. If Sterling finds those records, he'll check mine as well as Towne's. Proving Towne's alive would get him his promotion, but so would proving I died. He'd be exonerating the cop everyone's hated since nineteen sixty-nine. He'd be a hero. There's no way he'd pass up the chance."

"Well, okay. So what are we going to do?"

"Let's go to the library. The real library. I want to see if there's anything in the newspaper reports that we don't know about."

"I wonder what happened to your car. I should've asked Sterling. Maybe I should call and ask him."

"No, let's check the newspapers. Someone in the police department had to be involved. I don't think it was Sterling, but why take a chance? What if what he's really trying to do is find out how much you know and whether or not you can implicate him?"

"God, Charlie, you're scaring me. You sure are the suspicious type, aren't you?"

"I'm a cop, that's all."

The trouble with Charlie saying "Let's do it" is that it meant I had to do it. We went to the main library downtown and I spent fifteen minutes figuring out how to use the microfiche machine. I didn't even know what microfiche *was* before that. I sat in front of the machine for an hour, reading the *Oak Valley Journal.*

The story was on the front page from June 9th until June 12th. There was a nice picture of Charlie looking real young in his patrolman's uniform with his hair clipped short and another one of him with long hair. There were pictures of Samuel Towne, too. The June 11 front page had a large picture of him, just his head and shoulders. It looked like it might have been a mug shot although he wasn't holding one of those signs with a number on it. He had dark hair, a grim mouth, a big nose, and a chin that looked a little weak to me, although it was hard to pay attention to anything but his eyes. There was something about them that made me think of Charles Manson's eyes. Crazy eyes. Duke was sort of a Manson nut, the way some people are Kennedy assassination nuts.

1969. The Year of Woodstock. The Year Men Walked On The Moon. But it was also The Year of Charles Manson. *It was just—what, Duke? a week before Woodstock?—when the Manson Family murdered Sharon Tate and those other people. Sharon Tate was an actress, Lizbet, real pretty and she was eight months pregnant when she was killed. It wasn't all good back then; it wasn't all Woodstock.*

Duke brushes that aside with a wave of his hand, leaving a trail of smoke in the air, and tells me about Manson holding up a newspaper at his trial. The headline said: NIXON DE-CLARES MANSON GUILTY. I guess maybe Manson hoped the judge would decide the headline would influence the jurors too much for him to get a fair trial, but they all said it wouldn't, so the trial went on. Nixon had to do some fast tap-dancing, though, and retract his statement. I guess it didn't look too good to have the President of the United States say someone was guilty when the trial wasn't even over. I mean, it's suppposed to be "innocent until proven guilty," right? Nixon was right, though, and Manson was found guilty and sentenced to the gas chamber. He's still alive though, still in prison, because the death penalty was outlawed before he could be executed.

I'd like to meet Manson, just once, just to talk to him. He'll be in jail the rest of his life and he didn't even do it, wasn't even there when the murders were committed.

They killed seven people, Duke.

I know that, Lady. Didn't say I wanted him freed, just said I'd like to meet him.

Seven people, Lizbet: Sharon Tate and four others at her house and then a couple named La Bianca later that night, shot them and stabbed them and used their blood to write graffiti on the walls, killed them for no reason at all. No reason at all.

Still, I'd like to meet him, just like to meet a man who has that kind of power over other people. The ones who killed Tate and the others, they were following orders. Manson's orders. What kind of man has so much power over people that they'll commit bloody murder on his say-so? I'd just like to meet him.

I didn't think I'd want to meet him, not then and not now. I zipped the microfiche past the picture of Samuel Towne. I didn't ever want to meet *him* either, not that I was likely to since he was dead. Then again ... I met Charlie, didn't I? After the 12th of June the story was mentioned on an inside page for a week or so, then there wasn't anything else until July 10th and that was just a small story about a fund-raising drive for the widows and children of the two cops who died.

Duke always used to say persistence pays and I guess he

was right. On August 5th a front-page headline said VEHICLE
SOUGHT IN TOWNE CASE LOCATED. The Towne case!
They could have at least called it the Bilbo case.

Charlie's old VW bug was found in a residential neighborhood in Oakland, a neighborhood of pretty unobservant people
from the sound of it. The car had been parked in the same
place since June and no one bothered to report it until August
when someone stole all four tires and one of the residents
called the cops to have it towed away. He said it was an eye-
sore. Even then, the cops didn't realize it was Charlie's car at
first because the license plates had been changed and it had
been painted dark green. The paint job was described as "un-
professional," which I guess meant someone did it with cans
of spray paint. Before that, it was yellow with flowers and
peace symbols and all kinds of hippie stuff painted on it.

"Well, that doesn't really help us, Charlie, but—"

"*Shhh.*"

"*Sorry. Whoever killed you drove out of the warehouse that night,
right? And the cops thought it was you leaving. And then he painted
the car and stole some license plates for it and ditched it in Oakland.
He must have had your body in the car. It doesn't say anything about
bloodstains. Maybe he put you in a plastic bag or something. That
car would stick out like a sore thumb up in my neighborhood, but I
don't suppose we'd find anybody now who remembers seeing it way
back then.*"

"*I doubt it. I bet he didn't drive it up there anyway. Too risky, a
car like that up in the Foothills. I bet he drove it away from the
warehouse and stashed it somewhere, a garage probably, where he
could paint it, and he transferred my body to another car to take it
up to the Foothills.*"

"*So this isn't really very helpful, is it?*"

"*Not really. We might as well go.*"

"Well, give me a couple more minutes. I want to see what happened to the little girl." I was talking about a story I'd got interested in. It started in the middle of July and was still on the front page. A three-year-old girl had disappeared and two weeks later she just all of a sudden showed up in her backyard early one morning. There were some articles about it until August 5th, then nothing. They never did figure out where she'd been or how she got back home. Weird. I shut off the machine and returned all the microfiche and we left.

I forgot to mention that Captain Sterling followed us to the library. Charlie had spotted him right away. When we left the library, his car was still parked at the far end of the parking lot, but it looked empty. I thought maybe he'd fallen asleep and was slouched down in the seat, but when I pulled out of the lot, I saw him coming down the street with a Styrofoam coffee cup in his hand. He stopped real quick when he saw my car.

"Wave to him," Charlie said, so I did and he started to wave back, kind of catching himself just as his arm moved, you know, then he just stood there and he was still standing there when I turned the corner. Charlie laughed. It really was kind of funny.

The library is only a few blocks from the police station and we had to pass it to go home. We were right in front of it when Charlie all of a sudden said, *"Look!"* He didn't exactly shout it, but he sounded urgent enough that I thought I was about to run into someone or something like that so I slammed on the brakes—the Porsche stops on a real thin dime—and the guy in the car behind me swerved and slammed on his brakes, which squealed something awful, and his car ended up partly in the lane for oncoming traffic and the car that was coming up in that lane screeched to a stop and the car behind that one ... well, you get the idea. The domino effect, right? There were cars all over the street and drivers hanging out their windows and shouting at me and each other and horns honking and, well, trust me, it was pretty embarrassing.

"Now look what you did, Charlie! What the hell did you yell at me for?" Miracle of miracles, nobody had actually collided with anyone else so I started the Porsche—I stopped so fast I didn't have time to put the clutch in and the engine stalled—and I had driven forward about ten feet when Charlie said, *"Turn in there. The parking lot."*

"For Pete's sake." I wanted to put some distance between me and all those angry drivers behind me, but it was hard to argue with Charlie so I turned into the municipal parking lot across the street from the police station. I took a ticket from the machine, the gate opened, and I drove on in and found a parking place. Charlie was busy craning his neck to stare out the back window. "What is it?" I asked.

"What's he doing here?"

"Who?"

"He was coming out the door of the police station. Hurry, we can't lose him." Charlie opened his door and got out. I scrambled out, too, and practically had to run to catch up with him. He was going to un-link us if he wasn't careful.

"Who, Charlie? Who is it?"

"My son."

Chapter Ten

I knew Charlie'd been dead for twenty-seven years, but he only looked a few years older than me so when he said *my son* I got this picture of a little blond boy in my mind. And when he said, *"There,"* and pointed across the street, it took me a minute to realize he meant the man in jeans and a white dress shirt who was getting into a blue car that was parallel-parked in the loading zone in front of the police station.

"Get his attention, Lizbet. Don't let him leave. We have to find out what he's doing here."

Get his attention? What was I supposed to do? Run out in the middle of the street and rip off my clothes? Jeez, but Charlie could be a little irritating. I ran into the street, dodged cars going both directions, and made it to the opposite curb just as Charlie's son started his engine. Fortunately, traffic was too heavy for him to pull out of the parking place right away. I ran down the sidewalk to the car, jerked the door open and sort of fell into the passenger seat.

Charlie's son looked a lot like Charlie, except his hair was short and darker, more of a dirty blond than a real blond like his father's hair. They were about the same age. Well, you know what I mean. He looked a little startled. I mean, who wouldn't if some strange woman suddenly tumbled into his car?

But then he smiled, and, oh, *god*, he had Charlie's smile. "If this is a car-jacking, you're supposed to get in the *driver's* side."

I was so flustered I couldn't think of a single thing to say. Except "um." I said it two or three times.

"You're also supposed to have a gun or knife or at least look threatening enough to make me get out. Works better at night, too. On a dark, deserted street."

"I'm not trying to steal your car."

"Good, because you aren't doing a very good job of it."

I giggled. He shut off the engine and turned toward me. "So if it isn't the car you want, it must be me." He smiled again. Oh, god, that smile.

"Tell him to get his brains out of his balls and find out what he's doing here."

That, I guess I don't have to tell you, was Charlie. He was in the back seat. I turned around to look at him. His son looked back, too, and raised an eyebrow at me. I turned back around. He said, "Were you trying to get away from someone? That's the police station right there. If someone was bothering you—"

"No, it's nothing like that."

"All right."

"What should I do, Charlie? Should I tell him I know who he is?"

"I don't know if that's a good idea. Find out what he's doing here."

"How?"

Before Charlie could answer, if he planned to answer at all, his son said, "Do you need a ride somewhere? I don't know my way around, but if you can provide directions, I'll take you."

"You're from out of town? Are you here on business?"

"Not exactly. Do you need a ride somewhere?" His mood seemed to change suddenly. He was staring straight out the windshield and drumming his fingers on the steering wheel.

"Actually, my mother told me never to accept rides from strange men."

"Your mother's a smart woman."

"She's dead." And for some idiotic reason, I started crying. I mean, for Pete's sake, Lady's been dead for *years* and all of a sudden I was bawling my head off. Charlie's son leaned over toward me and murmured something about being sorry and patted my shoulder and tucked a handkerchief into my hand and patted my shoulder some more and somehow I kind of leaned over toward him and then I had my head on his shoulder and his arms were around me. And I heard a sigh—a real exasperated sigh—from the back seat.

I sat up straight and said, "I'm sorry, I don't know why I'm crying. My mother—"

And then this voice absolutely *roared,* "YOU LYING SON OF A BITCH!" I jerked around toward the sound. There was a man standing on the sidewalk right by the car. I couldn't see his face until I ducked my head down. Captain John Sterling. And did he look pissed.

Charlie's son was leaning over, looking out my window. "What the hell are you yelling about, Sterling?"

Sterling was leaning down to look in the car by then, his face close to mine and very red. "You lying son of a bitch! Never heard of her, huh? You bastard! If you weren't a cop, I'd arrest you right now for obstructing justice! You son of a bitch! I'm going to get you! I'm going to get *both* of you!" He pounded his fist on the top of the car then spun around and practically ran into the police station.

"What the hell?" Charlie's son said.

"What a mess," Charlie said.

"You're a cop, too?" I said.

Charlie's son was staring at me. I had the feeling he'd hit

the rewind button in his mind and was replaying Sterling's words. "Who are you?" he asked.

"Um."

He grabbed my wrist and held it like he expected me to try to get out of the car and run. "What's your name?"

"Um."

"Answer him, Lizbet. He's already figured it out anyway."

"Lizbet. Lizbet Lange."

He kept staring at me for a long time. He was breathing hard, like he'd been running, and he still had a death-grip on my wrist. Finally, he said, "Well, well, well."

"You're hurting my wrist."

He let go, real quick, like my skin had suddenly burned his hand.

"Where's my father?" he asked and, I couldn't help it, I started crying again. Not about my mother. About his father. Who was dead. And who was sitting in the back seat.

Chapter Eleven

I probably would have cried for an hour—I get on these crying jags every once in a while and I can go on practically forever—but Charlie kept telling me to calm down because we needed to find out what his son was doing in town and his son kept telling me to stop crying because he wasn't falling for *that* trick a second time. Lady was right: Men! That's what she always used to say, and she was right. Men!

They both made me so mad, my tears dried up. I pulled down the sun visor to see if there was a mirror on it. There wasn't, which was probably just as well. I was pretty sure my mascara was all over my face and I knew for sure that my eyes were red and puffy and my mouth always gets smeary-looking when I cry.

"You must not be married, huh?"

"Why? Because I'm not taken in by a few tears?"

"Because you don't have a mirror on your visor. What's your name anyway?"

"Don't you know?"

"How would I know?"

"Didn't my father tell you? Or has he forgotten I even exist?"

I chewed on my lip for a moment, trying to figure out

how to handle that one. I glanced over my shoulder at Charlie, but he wasn't much help. All he said was, *"You can't tell him about me, Lizbet. Not ever."*

"Listen, whatever your name is, I have never ever seen your father in the flesh." Well, that was true, wasn't it? "I've seen his picture, though. In some old newspapers. That's why I knew who you were. You look a lot like him. And I've never talked to him on the phone or gotten a letter from him, either." True, too, right?

"Then why did Sterling call me and ask if I knew you? He thinks you've been in contact with my father."

"Is that all he told you?"

"He said you slipped up and mentioned Charlie Bilbo in front of some cops and then you were stuck with explaining how you knew his name so you claimed to be psychic and told them a skeleton that turned up in your backyard was his."

"Well ... that's not exactly how it happened."

"Close enough," Charlie said. *"Don't confuse the issue."*

"So what did happen?"

"Something like that, I guess. What's your name?"

"Consult your crystal ball."

My crystal ball was on the blink: Charlie refused to tell me. "No earthly explanation" and all that.

"But, Charlie, just imagine the look on his face ... "

"Absolutely not, Lizbet. He wouldn't think you're psychic anyway. He'd just be convinced you've been in contact with me."

Charlie's son said, "This is the first time in twenty-seven years there's been any kind of lead about my father's whereabouts and I intend to find out what you know about him."

I sighed. "What I know won't help you. Look, my car's across the street. I'd really like to go home. My face is a mess and I'm starving to death. You can follow me if you want to."

He thought that over, probably trying to figure out if I was smart enough to lose him in traffic. He must have decided I wasn't. "Which car?"

"It's in the lot. A red Porsche."

"That figures. Sterling called you a rich bitch."

"Someday I'm going to punch Sterling right in the nose and if you aren't careful, you'll be next on the list." I got out of the car and slammed the door as hard as I could.

By the time I pulled up to the parking lot exit to pay the attendant, Charlie's son was waiting in the no-parking zone on the street. His car was in my rearview mirror all the way home.

"Wow," he said when we were in the house.

"I inherited it."

"You don't seem like the spoiled rich-kid type somehow."

I supposed that was a compliment, in a way. "My parents weren't rich. My ex-husband left it to me." I led him into the other living room, the one I like, with all the puffy pillows on the furniture. The drapes were open, giving us a view of the brick patio and the churned-up dirt in the backyard. The yellow crime scene ribbon was still sagging between stakes they'd stuck into the ground, but the cops must have finished for the day because the patrol car wasn't out front. I told Charlie's son I'd be right back and I went upstairs, with Charlie right behind me, of course.

I told him to go away. I felt pretty ragged so I decided to take a quick shower. Afterwards, I dressed in jeans and an oversized pink T-shirt with absolutely nothing written on the front and I didn't even bother drying my hair or putting on makeup.

I tingled while I was walking downstairs.

"I feel awful, Charlie. He thinks you're still alive. He's probably been searching for you his entire life."

"It's better for him to find out the truth."

"But I can't tell him the truth. He'll never know unless someone proves the bones are yours. He's just going to go on and on thinking you abandoned him."

"Then we'll have to prove they're mine, won't we?"

That was one of those things that sound easier said than done.

Charlie's son wasn't in the living room. I didn't have any trouble finding him though. I just followed a wonderful smell to the kitchen.

"I hope you don't mind," he said. "You said you were starving."

I couldn't believe he'd actually found something to cook, but he had. He was making scrambled eggs, with cheese and onion. My stomach growled.

"Must be the cook's day off, huh?"

"I don't have a cook."

"Why not?"

I told him. And then I rattled on and on while the eggs cooked and all the time we were eating. I told him about Duke and Lady and how they died and Tom and Tom's fortune and how I'd ended up with it and pretty soon I was telling him all this really personal stuff about how I don't have any friends now that I'm rich because my old friends are uncomfortable around me or else they want me to give them money to set them up in business and how I don't feel comfortable with rich people and how it was really lonely living here by myself and on and on and on and on. It was pathetic, but I couldn't seem to stop talking. Partly I think I kept going on and on because it was so weird to be sitting there with Charlie's son while Charlie himself was sitting next to me, eating my eggs and watching us.

Charlie's son didn't say much, mostly he just listened and

nodded every once in a while. I felt better when I finally wound down. Nothing perks you up like dumping all over someone else. While we were adding the dishes to the collection in the dishwasher, he suddenly said, "Jonathan Dillon."

"Huh? Oh, your name. Jonathan Dillon ... not Bilbo?"

He shook his head. "My mother took back her maiden name when she divorced him and changed mine, too."

"I guess she must've been pretty upset about the whole thing. Everyone was sure he bombed that building and killed those cops."

"She loved him. She couldn't believe he did it at first, but as time passed and he didn't get in touch with her, she decided everyone was right. She was bitter for a long time. She got married again when I was six and that helped some, I guess."

The kitchen was all cleaned up so we went back into the living room. I curled up at one end of the couch and Jonathan sat at the other end, turning a little to face me and draping his arm along the back of the couch.

"How old were you when Charlie died? I mean disappeared."

"I was almost three. Why do you think he's dead?"

Because his ghost is standing beside me. But I couldn't say that, could I? So I just shrugged and said, "It's just a feeling I have."

"I can't figure out your angle at all."

"I don't have an *angle*. I just ... I just ... I got interested in the case, that's all. I read all about it at the library and it just struck me as weird that Charlie would disappear so completely and it occurred to me that maybe he didn't, maybe he died and his body was never found."

"So you decided to claim some old bones in your backyard are his? That's pretty farfetched, Lizbet. I've been over and over all the information on the case and there's nothing to connect my father or Samuel Towne or SAMIC with this house or even this neighborhood."

"Any ideas, Charlie? None of this makes any sense unless I give him some reason why I think the bones are yours."

"Sorry, Lizbet, I can't help you."

I'd already noticed that on a number of occasions. What on earth good is a ghost anyway?

"I have a reason to think the bones are his, but I can't tell you what it is."

"Why not?"

"Because ... because it could be dangerous."

Jonathan laughed. *"You're* protecting *me?* I think I can probably handle danger a little better than you can."

"Oh, really?" I leaned toward him a little. "Don't underestimate me just because I'm a woman. I can take care of myself."

He held his hands up, palms toward me, like he was protecting himself. "Whoa, Lizbet. I didn't mean to make any generalizations about women. I just meant that I'm a cop and you're not and cops are trained to handle dangerous situations. No offense intended. My partner's a woman. I'd rather have her covering me than a lot of male cops I know."

"Where do you work anyway?"

"San Jose. That's where my mother moved when she left here. I've lived there ever since."

"How did Sterling know you're Charlie's son?"

"I met him seven or eight years ago, right after I became a cop. When I was kid, I never thought about my father much. I was so young when he disappeared that I don't have any real memories of him. I just knew what my mother told me and what I heard from other people. Mom kept in touch with his relatives, my grandparents especially, so I knew about him, I just didn't remember him and I wasn't particularly interested in him. I never thought about trying to find him or anything like that.

"Then I became a cop and found out that every cop in the state knows who Charlie Bilbo is. They all hate him. They use him as an example of the very worst kind of cop—the kind who'd sacrifice his own partners for money. It was hard, listening to them rehashing the case, knowing it was my father they were talking about. When word finally got out that I was his son, I had a couple run-ins with cops who didn't want to work with me. Because of him. Stupid, huh? Like being a crooked cop is a genetic trait. That all blew over, though. But I got interested in the case then. I guess at first I had some crazy idea I could clear his name. I came here—to the Oak Valley Police Department—to find out all I could about the case. Sterling's the one I talked to."

"Lucky you. He's a jerk."

Jonathan smiled. "Yeah, he is kind of, but he's a good cop. He's being considered for Deputy Chief."

And he was hoping to make it over Charlie's dead body.

"I've got a whole briefcase full of information about the case. Sterling gave me copies of all the reports, plus my mother saved all the newspaper and magazines articles. I've been over it and over it and I can't come up with anything that suggests it didn't happen just the way they think, that my father took the money and ran. I don't really care that much. I never thought about searching for him or anything like that, but when Sterling called ... I guess if there's a chance I could find him ... He is my father."

"I'll make you a deal, okay?"

"What kind of deal?"

"You show me all the stuff you have, and I'll tell you everything I know. Only I won't tell you why I think the bones are Charlie's, because I can't. I can't explain why, I just can't."

"Sounds to me like I'm getting the short end of the stick."

"You are, because I really don't know anything except what was in the newspapers and what Sterling told me."

Jonathan laughed. "You drive a hard bargain, Lizbet. Hell, why not? My only option is to try to force you to tell me and torturing women isn't my thing. Not," he hurried to add, "that I'm implying I could overpower you just because I'm a man and you're a woman. I realize you'd probably lick me in a fair fight so I'd have to sneak up behind you or something."

I bit my lip to keep from laughing. He could have knocked me down with a slap, but I thought it was kind of cute of him to be so, well, sensitive about women's feelings. I've been pawed and pinched and groped enough times to know that there are plenty of men out there who think women *exist* just for them to overpower.

"So you'll show me all the stuff you have? I can come to your house if you want."

"No need to. It's all in my briefcase in the car."

Chapter Twelve

Jonathan's briefcase was stuffed with papers, so we moved into the dining room where we had plenty of table space, *plenty* meaning seating for twelve. I sat at the head of the table in the big chair with a carved back and arms and Jonathan sat to my right on the side of the table in a slightly smaller chair with a carved back but no arms. I don't know why the person at the head of the table gets arms. Or a bigger chair. Charlie stood behind me, looking over my shoulder.

I looked at the police reports first. There was a stack at least an inch high but I figured out in a hurry that most of it was the same stuff over and over. Every cop who worked on the case filed a report so it was the same story in different words. Not that different of words, either. The cops all sounded pretty much the same, tossing in *perpetrator* and *victim* and *suspect* and *prior to* and *at that point in time* and *this officer* like the sell-by date on those words was about to expire and they wanted to be sure they used them up first. A lot of the reports were handwritten. Cops don't spell very good and their handwriting is awful. But I guess if they were Einsteins, they wouldn't be cops, right? Maybe not Einstein, I think he had dyslexia or something. But you know what I mean.

Most of the typewritten reports were summaries of the

whole case. I only found out a couple things that Sterling or Charlie hadn't already told me. One was that the big door at the warehouse had some kind of industrial-strength automatic garage door opener so all you had to do to open the door was flip a switch. Samuel Towne's body—or the body that was identified as Samuel Towne, anyway—was found at the foot of the wall where the switch was. So I guess he opened the door. Well, of course, right? Except for the cops he was the only one in the building.

The other new thing was that the name of the terrorist who was paying Samuel Towne for the kidnapping was Ivan Kosvak.

"Ivan! Jeez, Charlie, a Russian?"

"Something like that. I never found out who he was working for, but it might have been the Soviets. The Cold War was going strong back then."

The cops who died were named John Pillman and Orlando Escobar. The bomb—all the cops called it the explosive device—was placed near the door so their bodies were in really bad shape. If the rest of the SWAT team hadn't seen them getting blown up, they probably never would have been identified. Three other cops who'd been approaching the door were injured but they lived. The blast blew them back away from the building so they were banged up but not burned. The warehouse didn't exactly burn to the ground, but it came close.

There was a typed paragraph signed by a cop named John Aguilar, who was one of the SWAT team's lookouts that night. It said that he was sure Charlie had been driving the Volkswagen when it came out of the warehouse at two o'clock. All the street lights in the area had been broken and there weren't any outside lights on the building, but the driver lit a cigarette just as he drove by and Aguilar said he'd seen his face clearly when the cigarette lighter flared. "There is no doubt in this officer's mind that the driver was Charlie Bilbo" is how he put it.

"I didn't know you smoked, Charlie."

"Gave it up when I died. Why's that in a report?"

He leaned over to read the statement. *"He sounds positive it was you,"* I said. *"Did one of the others look a lot like you?"*

"He saw what he expected to see. It was pitch black that night and he was across the street. He might've lied, too. Maybe he was taking a leak or nodded off or something and didn't want anyone to know. Aguilar was a real flake. I never trusted him to cover my back."

I read some official-looking reports about Samuel Towne. The letterheads and signatures had all been blacked out so I suspected Sterling wasn't supposed to give them to anyone. They were probably FBI reports.

Samuel Towne was your general all-around bad boy. He was only twenty-four in 1969 but he'd been busy. He had a juvie record that made mine look pretty Mickey Mouse. Driving under the influence, joyriding, possession of a controlled substance, possession of stolen property, possession of an illegal firearm, destruction of public property, destruction of private property. He either cleaned up his act when he turned eighteen or he learned not to get caught. The juvie record was the only police record he had. He graduated from high school with a D average, but his SAT scores were so high Oak Valley College accepted him on a probationary basis anyway. He only took a couple classes each quarter so in 1969 he had just become a senior. There wasn't any mention of a job, so I don't know what he was doing the rest of the time. Masterminding the revolution, I guess. He'd been connected with a couple other student activist groups before SAMIC was formed.

A lot of the papers were surveillance reports. The local cops and the FBI spent a year and a half trying to catch

Towne doing something they could arrest him for. There were reports about the bank bombings they suspected SAMIC was responsible for and there was a long report about Charlie's undercover investigation and the plans for the bust.

There were also reports by the bomb squad and the fire department and the arson investigator and the medical examiner and on and on. It would take a week to read them all, so I moved on to the stuff Jonathan's mother had kept. Jonathan's mother, Charlie's wife. Ex-wife. No, his widow.

There was a photo album that could rip your heart right out. It started with Jonathan's birth certificate and newborn picture and went through baby pictures and birthday pictures and Christmas pictures and ended with a photograph Jonathan told me was taken the day before Charlie disappeared.

A neighbor had taken the picture. Charlie and his wife were sitting close together on the lawn in their backyard. Charlie looked just the same, long blond hair with the leather thong, sandals, jeans, and the silver and turquoise peace symbol on a chain around his neck. The only difference was that he wearing a tie-dyed T-shirt and no vest.

His wife was just a tiny bit on the plump side, with sandy hair and blue eyes and big dimples in her cheeks. She was wearing white shorts and a pink sleeveless top. She was holding Jonathan, a chubby toddler with pale hair and bright blue eyes and a scab on one knee.

They were all smiling and they all looked happy.

"What's your mother's name?" I asked Jonathan, mostly because I couldn't think of anything else to say.

"Amanda Reynolds."

I nodded and closed the photo album and picked up another album that had SCRAPBOOK printed on the front. It was full of newspaper clippings and magazine articles. Some of the newspaper clippings were the ones I'd read that morning. If I'd met Jonathan first I wouldn't have had to mess with that microfiche machine. There were also articles from other newspapers, mostly in this part of California, but some from L.A. papers and out-of-state papers.

Stories from two sleazy tabloids were the most interesting to read, which I guess doesn't say much about my taste in reading, but I can't help it. They were real tear-jerkers, with all this stuff about Charlie being the perfect husband and father and then his poor wife had to cope with him being a traitor and disappearing, leaving her with a little boy to raise all by herself. One of the tabloids had printed the picture from the photo album, the one with Charlie and his wife sitting on the lawn. It was black and white and grainy.

The same picture was also printed in color in a magazine. I stared at the picture for a long time. I had that weird *déjà vu* feeling again. Of course, I *had* seen the picture before, twice in the last thirty minutes. There was something ... but the feeling went away.

"Well," I said to Jonathan and Charlie, "there really isn't anything to go on is there?"

"Not really."

"What are you trying to find anyway? I told you everything supports the official conclusion. Charlie Bilbo killed Samuel Towne, stole the money, blew up the building, and was never seen again."

"It didn't happen that way."

"And you're not going to tell me what makes you think that, are you?"

"No. That was the deal, remember?"

"Yeah, that was the deal." He gathered up all the papers and started shoving them into the briefcase. I could tell he was mad, or at least disappointed, but there wasn't much I could do about it.

"I'm sorry. I'd tell you if I could."

He gave me a bleak smile. "Sure you would. There's some real good reason why you're running around trying to convince the cops my father's dead. Couldn't be that Sterling's right and you're Charlie Bilbo's girl and you're trying to make sure no one finds him."

"*What?* Are you crazy? For Pete's sake, he'd be *old.*"

"Only fifty-four. How old did you say that old geezer you married was?"

I opened my mouth, then closed it. What could I say?

"Okay if I use your phone?"

"Help yourself."

He was only on the phone for a minute. He told someone he was taking another couple days of personal leave. When he hung up, he said, "How about showing me where the guest room is."

"What? You can't stay here."

"Why not? Not enough room?"

"There's isn't any reason for you to stay here."

"I'm not letting you out of my sight, Lizbet. The only way you're going to get rid of me is to call the cops. But you won't do that, will you? Sterling's already on your case. Last thing you want's more cops, right? I'm not leaving. Either call the cops or show me to my room."

I showed him to a room, the bedroom farthest away from mine. It has a four-poster bed and it's all done in deep blue and cream, kind of an old-fashioned style. The cleaning people Tom hired still come every Thursday and they keep all the beds made up and towels in the bathrooms and stuff like that. "Nice," Jonathan said, "and to think I was going to get a room at Motel Six if I needed to stick around."

I walked out of the room and hurried downstairs, Charlie right on my heels. *"What are we going to do now? He's going to stay here until he figures out what I'm up to. And I don't even know what I'm up to. This is a real mess, Charlie. First Captain Sterling's following me and now I've got your son—another cop!—living in my house."*

"If you don't want him here, call the cops and have them throw him out. Tell them he's trespassing."

I stopped so fast I'm surprised Charlie didn't run into me. *"Is that what you want me to do?"*

"No, but you're a free agent, Lizbet. Do whatever you want."

I stared at him. *"I thought the whole point was that I'm your agent. Are you telling me I can just say I don't want to help you? Can I just tell you to go away?"*

"Of course you can."

But, of course, I couldn't. I sighed loudly. *"You know, Charlie, I always knew the past would come back to haunt me. But I thought it would at least be my own past."*

Chapter Thirteen

Jonathan went out to his car and brought in a suitcase, then he wandered through the house, poking around like he was thinking about buying it. I ignored him as much as I could. I'd been so busy with Charlie I hadn't paid any attention to my own life in two days. Not that my life needs a lot of attention.

I walked out to see if there was any mail. I hardly ever get anything except junk mail and stuff I order from some real classy mail-order catalogs. All the bills go to my financial manager and he sends me a report once a month.

I had a postcard from Scotland from my Grandma Rose— Lady's mother. She always wanted to go there, so I talked her into letting me pay for a trip. She's been kinda blue since Grandpa Bill died last year. Actually, she's been kinda blue since Lady died. First her daughter died and then her husband, all in two years. The postcard said "Having a great time. I may never come home!"

Hearing from Grandma Rose reminded me that I hadn't called Grandma and Grandpa Dutton lately. They're Duke's parents and they still live in Gilroy. I curled up in a chair in the casual living room and talked to them each for a few minutes. We're getting along pretty good now, but they didn't talk to me for a long time after I married Tom. I don't think they'll ever forgive me for that and they seem to think it's really weird that he left me his money. I think they think I must have been really good in bed, doing things nice girls don't do, because why else would a man leave all his money to me? But they're my grandparents so I try not to let it bother me too much.

Neither of them mentioned the skeleton so I guess it didn't make the Gilroy newspaper. They don't watch television except for professional wrestling and old movies, Fred Astaire and Ginger Rogers mostly. Grandma Dutton says everything else on television, even the news, is nothing but sex and violence. So she watches half-naked men with oiled muscles prancing around a ring and putting choke holds on each other. Go figure.

I looked through a new lingerie catalog, but nothing really appealed to me. What's the point in wearing pretty undies if no one ever sees you in them? I stuck the catalog in a drawer so Jonathan wouldn't see it. Charlie, of course, had stood right beside me while I leafed through it, but he didn't say anything.

I asked him again what we were going to do, but he didn't have any ideas. *"If Sterling finds the dental records and they identify your bones, the cops'll be pretty interested in finding out what really happened that night, won't they?"*

"Maybe. It was a long time ago. Unless they come up with a new lead, there isn't much they can do."

"So we have to find a new lead, right?"

"That would help. Otherwise, they're going to be putting some pressure on the one thin lead they have."

"What's that?"

"You."

"Oh, *shit.*" I said that out loud, and Jonathan poked his head into the room and said, "What's wrong?"

"Nothing. I chipped a nail."

He went away, headed toward the kitchen. I picked up the morning paper, which I hadn't looked at yet. There was just a little bitty paragraph on the first page of the local news about the cops trying to identify the skeleton. I almost skipped an article with the headline WOMAN ASSAULTED IN HOME but a name in it kind of jumped out at me: Yakamoto.

"Charlie, listen to this. 'Betty Yakamoto, forty-eight, of Fourteen Ninety-eight South Twelfth Street, was hospitalized after being struck over the head by an unseen assailant in her home. The attack occurred at eight p.m. last night when Yakamoto returned home and apparently interrupted a burglary in progress. The suspect fled after attacking Yakamoto with a blunt object. Police are investigating.' Yakamoto! That can't be a coincidence. Oh, jeez, Charlie, you don't think Sterling..."

"Not likely. He can get the dental records legally. Why would he try to steal them? It's interesting, though. It means there's another player in the game." Charlie laughed. *"You know what Sterling's going to think? That I did it. I'm surprised he hasn't stormed over here already."*

"Oh, god, he'll think I'm mixed up in it. Look, maybe it's just a coincidence. I mean, there are eight Yakamotos in the phone book. It doesn't have to be the same woman."

"That's a little too coincidental for me, but it wouldn't hurt to find out for sure. Call the hospital and see if you can talk to her."

"I don't want to talk to her! I don't even know her. What on earth would I say?"

"I'm sure you'll think of something."

Jeez.

I thought of a whole pack of lies. Mrs. Yakamoto had eighteen stitches in her head but was doing fine and she was going to be released in the morning. She was tickled pink to talk to a reporter who was getting more information for an in-depth story about the attack. She told me all about walking into her house and getting bashed over the head before she could even turn the light on. She hadn't caught even a glimpse of whoever attacked her. As far as she knew nothing had been taken. The cops told her it looked as if the burglar was searching through her closets.

She was employed by a dentist named Robert Richards. She'd worked in his office for nine years and before that she spent ten years working for James McMillan, Charlie's dentist. "I worked for him right up 'til the day he died. The poor man just didn't wake up one morning. Such a nice man, too."

"That must have been rough on his patients. I mean, some of them would be right in the middle of treatments. What happened to them? Their records and things like that?"

Mrs. Yakamoto didn't seem to realize we'd gotten off the subject of the attack. "Oh, they just picked another dentist and I sent all the paperwork wherever they told me to. I spent over a month taking care of all that after Dr. McMillan passed away."

"What about patients he hadn't seen in a while? Suppose a patient hadn't been to see him for years and all of a sudden decided to make an appointment. Would their records still be on file?"

"Oh, Dr. McMillan was a real pack rat. He never got rid of anything. Cleaning out his office was a real chore."

"What did you do with them?"

"With what?"

"The old files. From patients he hadn't seen in a long time."

Mrs. Yakamoto was silent. I was holding the receiver so tight my fingers ached. After a moment, I said, "Mrs. Yakamoto?"

"That's the same thing the policeman asked me."

"Oh?"

"Just a little while ago. A policeman came to see me. Captain ... something, I forget. He wanted to know if I had the old dental records. Now why on earth would he think I'd keep something like that all these years?"

"So you don't have them?"

"Of course not. What use would they be? I don't even know what happened to them. I took care of sending the active files to other dentists. Mandy cleared out all the old files. I don't know what she did with them."

"Who's she?"

"His assistant. I was his secretary and receptionist."

"Do you remember her last name?"

"It's been years. Mandy ... Oh, I can't think of it. Poor thing, there was a big scandal. I've forgotten the details. It was way before I went to work for Dr. McMillan. Her husband was with the police and he did something wrong, killed someone I think, and disappeared. Poor thing, she had a child to support and it was a big scandal, whatever her husband did. She had to change her name, it was so bad. She got married again later and her name—Reynolds! That's it! Mandy Reynolds. What is this all about? Why are the police interested in those old records? I don't understand what this has to do with—"

"My other line's ringing, Mrs. Yakamoto. Will you please hold on for a minute?" I hung up.

"*Well?*" Charlie asked.

"*You didn't tell me your wife worked for James McMillan.*"

"*She did? Must have been after I died. She was a dental assistant, but she worked for a guy named Peters. She wanted me to start seeing him, but I'd been going to McMillan all my life so I stuck with him. Did Mrs. Yakamoto know where the files are?*"

"No. She said Mandy—*your wife*—took care of all the old files when he died."

"Did she?"

"Charlie, doesn't it seem ... well, a little coincidental that your wife went to work for Dr. McMillan?"

"Not really. She probably changed jobs after I died to get away from people who knew about me. She changed her name ..."

"And moved away. That's what you told me."

"I thought she did. She's in San Jose now. I guess I thought she moved there then. My knowledge of things that happened after I died is pretty skimpy."

"Oh, yeah, I forgot—she did move. Jonathan said so. She must have commuted to work."

"It's only what? Twenty-five or thirty miles, something like that. She knew Dr. McMillan because I went to him. Maybe there weren't any jobs available in San Jose and he had an opening. He probably felt sorry for her and wanted to help her out. With her name changed, his patients wouldn't be likely to know who she was. There weren't any pictures of her in the papers, just that one in the tabloids and who reads them?"

"Lots of people, but I don't guess they'd recognize her. I don't think I'd recognize my dentist's assistant if I saw her somewhere else. I'm not even sure I'd recognize my dentist. I keep my eyes closed as much as I can."

"Well, it looks like the dental records are a dead end. It may not be possible to prove the body's mine after all."

"Your wife should know what happened to them. I don't suppose you know her husband's first name."

"How would I know his name?"

"I guess I could ask Jonathan."

"I don't think it's a good idea to let him know what you're trying to do. Especially if it involves his mother in any way."

"Not to worry, Charlie. Subtlety is my middle name."

I found Jonathan slouched down on the couch in the

formal living room with his feet on the coffee table and his hands clasped behind his head. "I see you're making yourself right at home."

"Why not?"

I wanted to say because it wasn't his home, but I kept my mouth shut. If I wanted information out of him, starting a fight wasn't the way to do it.

Charlie stayed by the door. I sat down next to Jonathan and started talking about Duke and Lady. Right out of the blue, I know, but I figured he wouldn't think anything about it since I already spilled my guts to him while we were eating. After a couple minutes I worked my way around to names. "A lot of people thought it was awful that I called my parents by their names. I always called them Duke and Lady even when I was a little kid. It never seemed funny to me, but I guess some people think it isn't respectful or something. What do you think?"

Jonathan shrugged. "Doesn't seem to me it matters what you called them as long as that's the way they wanted it."

"What about you? What do you call your mother?"

"Mom."

I nodded. "Mom. And you called Charlie 'Dad,' I suppose, or 'Daddy.'"

"I don't remember." He swung his feet off the table and sat up straight.

"I guess not. You were pretty young. What about your stepfather ... um, what was his name?"

"Reynolds. I called him Dad."

"Did you? Some people call their stepparents by their first names. Called? Did he die?"

"They got divorced a while back."

"Oh. I'm sorry. So I guess you don't call him Dad any-more, do you? Is that the way it works with stepparents? I mean, I guess he didn't adopt you or your last name would be Reynolds instead of Dillon. So you aren't really related anymore, are you? So what do you call him now?"

"I believe the last time I saw him I called him a motherfucking cocksucker. Which was at least half true."

"Oh."

He brushed his hair back off his forehead and said, "What are you after, Lizbet? My mother's phone number? She got divorced four or five years ago. Her phone's listed under A. M. Reynolds. If you'd asked, I'd have given it to you, but you can just call Information now. Her ex-husband's first name is George. He moved to San Diego last I heard. If you want to talk to him, call all the bars in town, he'll be in one of them."

Charlie was laughing. I got up and stalked out of the room without looking at either of them. Men!

Chapter Fourteen

I got Amanda Reynolds's phone number from Information but when I called, I got an answering machine. I couldn't think of a message so I just hung up.

I called Yung Sun's and ordered dinner. Yung Sun's has great food, but it takes at least an hour and a half for the food to arrive at the door. It was almost seven and I was starving so I drank a Pepsi and ate some pretzels. I was sitting at the kitchen table with one hand holding up my head, stuffing pretzels into my mouth one after the other, when Jonathan joined me. Helping himself to a handful of pretzels, he said, "What do you want with my mother?"

"I want to check you out. I only have your word for it that you're a cop. You could be an escaped convict for all I know. I plan to lock my bedroom door tonight."

He pulled out his wallet and showed me his driver's license and his police shield.

"Where's your gun?"

"In an ankle holster."

"Really? Let me see."

He wasn't kidding. He really did have a gun in an ankle holster. "Guns turn you on?" he asked.

"No. Neither do most men."

"What does?"

I suddenly thought of my fantasy last night—with Charlie in it—and felt myself blush. "It's none of your business."

"Okay. What do you want with my mother?"

"She worked for Dr. McMillan."

"McMillan? Yeah, she worked there for years, until he died. So what?"

"He was Charlie's dentist. The dental records were switched, Jonathan. The ones Sterling showed me aren't Charlie's and unless Dr. McMillan's old records are still around somewhere there's no way to prove the cops have the wrong x-rays and no one will ever believe the bones are his."

"How do you know they were switched?"

"I told you: Because the ones Sterling has with Charlie's name on them aren't Charlie's."

"How do you know that?"

"I just do. Why would I want to find them if I didn't know the cops have the wrong ones?"

"I don't have any idea. Nothing you do makes much sense to me."

"Well, it would if you'd just believe me. Your father died, Jonathan. I'm sorry, but he did. And he was buried in my backyard. And whoever killed him is the one who blew up the building and stole the money. All these years everyone's thought Charlie was a traitor and a killer, but he wasn't." I sniffled and wiped my eyes on my sleeve. Jeez, every time I turned around I was crying. "I don't know what's the matter with me. Everything's so mixed up. Don't worry, I'm not going to start bawling my head off again." I stood up. "Listen, I want to lie down for a few minutes. I ordered Chinese. Will you get the door when it comes? There's money in the top drawer in the chest in the front hall. Give the guy a big tip, too."

I started to walk past him but he grabbed my wrist. He was looking at me with a strange expression. "You're not lying, are you? You really believe those bones are his." He slid his hand around so he wasn't holding my wrist but my hand.

I nodded. "But I can't tell you why."

He held my hand for a moment longer, his thumb kind of massaging the back of my hand. "I'll let you know when the food gets here."

As I walked past Charlie, he grinned and said, *"Is that romance I detect in the air?"*

"Oh, drop dead, Charlie."

I didn't plan to fall asleep, but I did. One minute I was looking at Charlie, who was standing at the foot of the bed, absently fiddling with his peace symbol, and the next thing I knew, Jonathan was leaning over the bed telling me it was time to eat. I sat up, feeling confused and groggy, not quite out of the dream I'd been having. The same dream again: I was back in the morgue, naming Charlie's things: *Charlie's vest, Charlie's sandal, Charlie's other sandal, Charlie's belt.* In the dream it seemed really important, urgent actually, like something bad would happen if I didn't name everything exactly right. Weird. I shook my head to clear it and told Jonathan I'd be down in a couple minutes.

We were filling our plates from the little white boxes when the doorbell rang. It's a real pretty chime and I always wonder for a moment what it is. It doesn't sound like a doorbell and since nobody visits me I haven't heard it often enough to get used to it. It chimed a second time just before I reached the entry. I peeked out the window. Captain John Sterling.

I thought about not opening the door, but since the Porsche and Jonathan's car were both parked in front of the house, it seemed kind of stupid. I didn't bother saying hello to him, though. I just opened the door and he walked in. "We're in the middle of dinner," I said and went back to the kitchen, with Sterling practically on my heels. And Charlie, of course.

"Hello, Sterling. What's up?" Jonathan said. He didn't seem upset to see him. I was a little nervous myself.

Sterling pulled out a chair and dropped into it. I sat next to Jonathan and finished fixing my plate. Sterling ignored Jonathan. He looked at me and said, "I'm tired."

What did he want from me? A bed? I took a bite of sweet and sour pork.

"I'm tired," he said again. "I went to a lot of trouble yesterday to track down Betty Yakamoto, the woman who worked in McMillan's office. It was pure luck that I even found out her name. You ever try to find out who worked for a dentist who's been dead for ten years?" He didn't wait for an answer. One of those rhetorical questions, I guess. "If her name was Smith, I'd still be looking for her."

Jonathan said, "What's your point, Sterling? Cops are overworked? Don't captains have flunkies around to do their drudge work for them in this town? Why are you bothering, anyway? You don't believe Lizbet, so why are you trying to find the records?"

Sterling gave him a dirty look. "The *point* is that the name of McMillan's secretary isn't something you just look up at the library. So what I want to know is, how did someone else find her before I did?"

Sterling was looking at me. I felt guilty. Cops always make me feel guilty. "I don't know," I said. Did that make it sound like I knew something I shouldn't know? It's so hard to know what to say to cops. "I saw the story in the paper."

"That wasn't any burglary. He was looking for something he thought she might have stored away. Like old dental records. I talked to her this afternoon. She doesn't know what happened to the files. Couldn't even remember the last name of the other woman who worked there."

I looked at Charlie, who shook his head, then at Jonathan, who looked completely innocent as he stuffed another forkful of egg fu yung in his mouth. Neither of us said anything. I don't know why exactly. I couldn't think of a good reason not to tell him that Jonathan's mother was the other woman in McMillan's office except, well, it just seemed like a real peculiar coincidence.

Sterling said, "I'm gonna find out what you two are up to if it's the last thing I do. I come across anything that connects you to Charlie Bilbo, Ms. Lange, I'm arresting you and your smartass boyfriend, too. Even if I can't make the charges stick, so what? You"—he pointed at Jonathan—"are gonna be trying to explain it to your Chief and you"—he pointed at me—"are gonna spend a few hours at least sitting in the dirtiest, smelliest jail cell I can find before you get some hotshot lawyer to spring you."

Jonathan laughed. I didn't see anything funny about it.

"I *want* you to find the dental records. There's no reason for me to try to find them myself and I wouldn't ever hit some poor woman over the head."

"Don't waste your breath, Lizbet. He's just blowing smoke."

I know an old joke about blowing smoke but it didn't seem like the right time to tell it. It's dirty anyway. *"Charlie, we want him to find the records. Why shouldn't I tell him about Jonathan's mother?"*

"Why do his job for him? Jonathan can ask her about the records and you'll be one step ahead of Sterling."

I didn't really want to be a step ahead of Sterling, I just wanted him to leave me alone. I said, "You must have told someone you were trying to find Mrs. Yakamoto."

Sterling shrugged.

"You did, didn't you? Who'd you tell? Don't you see? Someone in the police department was involved, otherwise whoever killed Charlie wouldn't have known the SWAT team was coming and there wouldn't have been any reason to rig up the bomb."

Both Captain Sterling and Jonathan stared at me. Jonathan frowned. Sterling said, "You're amazing, Ms. Lange. First you got a dead cop in your backyard, now you got a whole conspiracy theory. All the money you got, you should be able to afford a shrink. I'd think about making an appointment if I were you."

Jonathan stood up suddenly. Sterling glanced at his face and stood up, too. Jonathan looked like he was thinking about punching Sterling's lights out. I got up quickly and said, "I'll show you to the door, Captain." Lady always said the only way to deal with rude people is to out-class them. I think that's the first time I ever managed to do it. Sterling looked like he was going to say something, then he just turned away and headed toward the front of the house. I gave Jonathan a smirky little smile on my way out of the room, just to let him know I didn't need him coming to my defense.

I watched Sterling drive off, then I hurried back to the kitchen and asked Jonathan if he would ask his mother about the dental records.

"She's on vacation."

"Well, no wonder she didn't answer. Why didn't you tell me?"

"You didn't ask. She's in an RV campground near Reno and I don't know its name. I'll call the police department there and see if I can talk someone into doing a favor for a fellow cop. Is that all you're working on? Old dental records?"

"Yes. Well, the landscaping company that put in the lawn here." I told him what Mrs. Altman had said about the condition of the yard the night Charlie died. "Someone knew it would be a good place to bury a body, so maybe someone working for the landscaping company was involved. I don't know if they'd know who was working for them that long ago, though."

"Well, I'll give it a shot. What's the name?"

Wouldn't you know I couldn't remember? Charlie said, *"Braverman's."*

"Braverman's," I said to Jonathan.

He spent almost an hour on the phone. I eavesdropped, but since I could only hear his half of the conversations, I still had to wait until he finished to find out what anyone said.

He got hold of Jacob Braverman, the old man who started the business. In 1969 he only had a handful of employees and they were all relatives of his. He remembered working on my house because of the big delay with the construction. He had scheduled the job several times and had to keep changing the date because there wasn't any point in doing landscaping when construction workers were stomping around all day. Then Mr. Altman insisted on having it done in a big hurry and Mr. Braverman already had plenty of other jobs lined up so he'd ended up hiring extra laborers for the Altman job. He told Jonathan he'd have to go through all the old records in his storeroom and he'd get back to him, probably by noon tomorrow. It's amazing how easy it is to get information when you can tell people you're a cop, although Jonathan didn't exactly specify what police department he worked for. Braverman had read about the skeleton being found so he wasn't even surprised about being asked.

A cop in Reno got a message to his mother and she called back in about twenty minutes. Basically, she said *Are you kidding?* when Jonathan asked if McMillan's dental records from twenty-seven years ago were still around. I think she also got upset, thinking Jonathan had decided to search for his father after all these years. He kept telling her it was something else entirely and she shouldn't worry about it.

"So the dental records are gone, right?"

"Those records would've been more than fifteen years old when McMillan died. She said if they didn't have any idea how to get in touch with the patient, they dumped them."

"So Charlie's and Samuel Towne's definitely would've been thrown out."

"Towne?"

I told him about Samuel Towne and Charlie going to the same dentist. "That's what Sterling's doing. He doesn't believe the bones are Charlie's, but he started thinking that maybe Samuel Towne's dental records were switched and he didn't really die in the explosion. He thinks if he can prove that, he'll get his big promotion."

"Ah. That explains what he's up to. I couldn't figure out why he was taking you seriously."

"I thought you said you believed me now."

"I'm willing to believe *you* believe the bones are my father's. But since you won't give me a good reason, I just have to assume you're ..."

"Crazy?"

"Obsessed."

"Obsessed! You do think I'm crazy!" I glared at him, which made him smile for some reason. It's hard to keep glaring at someone who's smiling at you with Charlie Bilbo's smile, so I said, "I'm tired and I'm going to my room. You can go to hell."

Chapter Fifteen

I watched television for a while, then I got ready for bed. I wasn't really sleepy so I propped myself up against a pile of pillows and worked on the crossword puzzle in the newspaper.

Charlie was sitting on the window seat, doing nothing, which is what he was always doing. I wondered if he got bored. Maybe time was different for him. He did help me with some of the crossword clues. I pointed out that there was no earthly explanation for me knowing that "nerve tissue" is "glia," but he just laughed and said no one was going to ask me how I knew.

"I just can't leave any loose ends behind when I leave, Lizbet."

"Well, then, you better come up with some way to explain how I knew your name."

"Don't worry about it. It'll all work out."

I sighed and turned to the "Tempo" section of the paper, which covers all the arts and entertainment news. I keep thinking I'll go to a play or a concert or something but I don't want to go alone. My social life really sucks. All the guys I used to know are either scared to death to talk to me or they want my money and I don't know how to meet guys in my own tax bracket. I don't even have any girlfriends anymore. I always thought whoever said money can't buy happiness was full of shit, but lately I've been wondering if there isn't a little bit of truth in it.

"Hey, look at this, Charlie. There's going to be a display of Horst Martinez's stuff at the Oak Valley College Art Center this coming weekend. Some of it's for sale. Maybe I should buy a wall decoration or something. I liked some of those metal sculptures in the book."

"Does he still live here?"

"Um ... no, it says he's a resident of Los Gatos. He taught at Oak Valley College when you knew him, right?"

"Yeah. He was a history professor. Art was just his hobby."

I yawned and said, "Maybe I'll go take a look at the display Saturday." I turned off the lamp, then moved some of the pillows from behind me and curled up on my side, wondering if Charlie would still be here Saturday. It seemed like he'd always been around and it was only yesterday that he showed up. Thinking about him leaving made me feel funny, not sad really, but a little scared. If he left and I never saw him again, it would be just like he died and I don't handle it real good when people I know die.

"Do you want me to go away until morning?"

"No. Stay here."

It took me a while to fall asleep. I kept looking at Charlie and wondering what Jonathan was doing and wondering if Captain Sterling was lurking around to see if I was going to sneak out of the house in the middle of the night and bash somebody over the head trying to find twenty-seven-year-old dental records.

I had that same dream again, just before dawn. The morgue was cold and brightly lit. *Charlie's vest, Charlie's sandal, Charlie's other sandal, Charlie's belt:* I named Charlie's things over and over and faster and faster until I felt positively frantic and I woke myself up.

It was way too early to get up, but I didn't think I'd be able to fall asleep again so I got up and put a robe on. I have all kinds of nightgown and robe sets. This one was white cotton with lots of lace. The woman at Madam and Eve's called it Victorian. I thought the Victorians were prudes, but I guess not. Charlie stood up. He didn't stretch or anything. He hardly ever did anything but just stand, except that sometimes he fiddled with his peace symbol. *"You're up early."*

"I had a bad dream."

"What was it about?"

"The morgue. I don't want to talk about it."

In the kitchen I fixed myself a cup of cocoa, zapping a mug of water in the microwave and then stirring the hot chocolate mix into it. I was all out of marshmallows and I didn't have any whipped cream, either. I sat on one of the stools at the counter and swiveled it around to face Charlie.

I thought that it must be a real time-saver not to have to bathe or shave or change clothes. He looked the same in the morning as he did at night. His hair didn't tangle up or look like it needed a wash. His whiskers didn't grow. He never changed: long blond hair, the leather thong across his forehead and tied at the back of his head, bell-bottom jeans, the blue chambray shirt, peace symbol, leather belt and vest and sandals. The leather belt and vest and sandals that were lying at the foot of his skeleton in the morgue. *Charlie's vest, Charlie's sandal, Charlie's other sandal, Charlie's belt.* Naming them had seemed so important in my dream. Maybe it was just because I hadn't told Sterling those were Charlie's things. But how could I explain knowing what Charlie was wearing when he died?

When he died! "Charlie! That's what you were wearing when you died, isn't it?"

He looked down, like he wasn't sure what he was wearing, then nodded.

"But it wasn't there."

"What are you talking about?"

"Your peace symbol. If you were wearing it that night, where is it? It wasn't in my yard. Are you sure you were wearing it?"

"Of course. This is exactly how I was dressed. I always wore it."

"Yeah, you had it on in that picture Jonathan showed me. So where is it? The cops've spent two days digging around out back. It wouldn't rot away, would it?"

"No. It's silver, it might tarnish, but it wouldn't rot."

"So why didn't they find it?"

"I don't know."

"Because whoever killed you took it! Why not? It's silver and maybe he even knew about Horst Martinez being written up in an art magazine and figured it would be worth a lot some day."

"Well ... that could be true, but unless he wears it out in public and we happen to see him ..."

"How many people knew Horst Martinez gave it to you?"

"Most of the people I knew, I suppose."

"The other cops?"

"Sure, they all knew."

"It would be worth a fortune today. Maybe whoever took it from you sold it to a museum or something. That book told where his stuff is displayed, didn't it? Some of it's in private collections, I remember that. I didn't look through the whole book, though. Maybe there's a picture of it in there."

I left my hot chocolate on the counter and we went into the library. I looked at every single page of *The Art Of Horst Martinez*. The only silver and turquoise peace symbol in the entire book was the one Horst Martinez was wearing in the picture of him sitting at his work table.

"Phooey," I said.

"Well, it was worth a shot."

I flipped through the pages, stopping at the picture of Martinez wearing his pendant. "Maybe he'd know who has it. If you owned something a famous artist made before he got famous would you tell the artist? You know, maybe write and say how much you liked it or something like that."

"I don't know. Maybe. Martinez wouldn't forget he gave it to me, though. If someone showed up with it after I disappeared, surely he'd question how they got it."

Well, that was true. I looked at the picture again, studying the peace symbol. I've always thought of it as rocketship shape in a circle but I know it's really a design based on semaphores. *It was designed by some pacifists in Britain, Lizzy-bit. They used the semaphores for the letters N and D, the first letters of the French words for "nuclear disarmament." You know what a semaphore is?* I say no and Duke explains that it's a method of communication, sort of like smoke signals, only it's done with flags. It used to be used on ships, with one ship semaphoring a message to another ship.

Two flags are held at different angles for each of the twenty-six letters of the alphabet. For the letter D, one flag is held straight up, the other straight down—*Think of it like the hands on a clock, Lizzy-Liz; one flag is at twelve o'clock, the other is at six o'clock.* For the letter N, the flags are held downward and slightly out from the body, one at four o'clock and one at eight o'clock. The peace symbol combines the two semaphores: a vertical line cuts through the center of a circle and two shorter lines radiate downward from the center of the vertical line.

The letters N and D stand for Nuclear Disarmament, which is probably something like *dees-ar-mah-mahn noo-clee-aire* in French. The only French I really know is *merci beaucoup.*

Speaking of French, I suddenly had that weird *déjà vu* feeling again. The pendant was in the photograph Jonathan showed me, of course. Charlie was wearing it when the picture was taken and he was wearing it now. And Horst Martinez was wearing one just like it.

Just like it. My stomach flopped over.

"Charlie! What if it's the same one? Martinez taught at Oak Valley College. Samuel Towne went to Oak Valley College. SAMIC was started at Oak Valley College. What if ... When was this picture taken?"

"Fairly recently. He was young, maybe twenty-five, in nineteen sixty-nine."

I checked the caption under the picture in *The Art Of Horst Martinez.* "It was taken in nineteen eighty-eight."

"Do you have a magnifying glass?"

I have one of everything. I found a magnifying glass in a desk drawer. Charlie took off his peace symbol and put it on the desk next to the book. The peace symbol in the picture was much smaller, of course, but the photograph was good, very clear and detailed. I studied the pendant through the magnifying glass for a long time, comparing it to Charlie's ghost pendant. "I'm sure it's the same one, Charlie. Take a look. Check out the hammer marks on the silver, and the stones—especially the stones. They're identical. Have you ever seen identical turquoises? It has to be the same one."

Charlie peered through the magnifying glass for a couple minutes. *"I think you're right. We need to find out how Martinez got hold of it."*

"How can we? He's a famous artist. He'll have an unlisted

phone number. The article in the paper said his studio is in his home. We'd have to drive down every street in Los Gatos and hope he has his name on the mailbox."

"Maybe Jonathan can get his address."

"Oh, yeah, good idea."

"What's a good idea? You always talk to yourself?" Jonathan was standing at the library door, wearing nothing but a pair of gray sweat pants. And I mean it was fairly obvious that he was wearing nothing else. I was all of a sudden very aware that I was naked under my nightgown and robe. I mean, of course, you're always naked under your clothes, but sometimes you're just more aware of it. Jonathan made me *very* aware of it.

"I was thinking out loud."

"Sounded like you were talking to someone. I thought you were on the phone."

"Well, I wasn't."

"So I see. Who's in Los Gatos?"

"Horst Martinez."

"The artist? Do you know him?"

"Of course not. But I need to talk to him. Do you think you can get his address for me?"

"Maybe. What do you want with him?"

I told him to get the photograph from his briefcase. He put on a white T-shirt before he came back. Too bad. "Look at Charlie's peace symbol. I thought it looked familiar and I suddenly remembered where I'd seen it." I showed him the picture in *The Art of Horst Martinez.* "Take a look, Jonathan. It's the same one."

After he'd examined the two pictures with the magnifying glass, he said, "Looks like they're the same. So what?"

"Charlie was wearing it the day before he died—when that picture of him and you and your mother was taken. I bet he always wore it. It was part of his hippie disguise. And almost twenty years after he died, Horst Martinez was photographed wearing it. How did he get it?"

"I remember it. It's the only real memory I have. I don't really remember him at all, but I remember playing with the peace symbol. He must have sold it or given it to Martinez or something."

"Come on, Jonathan, he was wearing it the day before he died. He was busy working on a big case. He wouldn't be running around giving away jewelry. I think he was wearing it when he was murdered and whoever killed him took it and somehow Horst Martinez ended up with it."

"I guess it wouldn't hurt to ask Martinez how he got it."

"Asking him flat-out how he got it back isn't a good idea. Why didn't he go to the cops? He knew I was missing."

"I can't tell Jonathan how you got it, can I? No earthly explanation, you know."

"Amanda knows."

"Why don't you ask your mother about it, Jonathan. If he always wore it and where he got it, stuff like that."

"I don't think that's necessary."

"Yes it is."

"Why?"

"Because ... because Horst Martinez and Samuel Towne and SAMIC were all connected to Oak Valley College. Maybe Martinez knew Towne. Maybe he was even involved with SAMIC. There has to be some kind of connection. He has a peace symbol that belonged to a murdered cop."

"A cop you claim was murdered."

"Oh, for Pete's sake. Okay, even if he wasn't murdered, even if he's alive now, it's still important. Martinez has Charlie's peace symbol. He had to get it after Charlie disappeared, so he either got it from someone else or from Charlie himself."

"Still, I don't see any reason to bother my mother. She's already upset because she thinks I'm trying to track my father down. Let's just talk to Martinez."

"Bad idea, Lizbet."

"No."

"No?" He raised an eyebrow at me. "I'll do it myself if you don't want to."

"You must not be a very good cop."

"What?"

"Because it's just plain stupid to let someone know you suspect them. Even I know that."

Jonathan seemed to have a hard time getting his teeth unclenched enough to talk. "I'm a good cop. There's no good reason to suspect Martinez of anything."

"What if I told you that I have Charlie's peace symbol, that it's right here in this room? Wouldn't you suspect me of knowing something about Charlie's death? Or his disappearance, if you prefer. You know you would. You'd be all over me trying to find out how I got the peace symbol. If I told Sterling I had it, he'd arrest me on the spot. So why is it different with Martinez? Because he's famous? Because he's a big important artist and I'm just a waitress who lucked into some money? Because he's a man?"

Jonathan took a couple of deep breaths. "I promise you it has nothing at all to do with Martinez being a man and you being a woman."

"Because he's famous then."

"Because there's no evidence ... Never mind. You're right. Martinez is now officially a suspect. I'll see if I can get an address for him. I'll get hold of my mother, too. She gave me the phone number for the RV-park manager. It's early enough she shouldn't have headed to the casinos yet."

He sat down at the desk and picked up the phone. I went back to the kitchen and re-zapped my hot chocolate. It really isn't very good without marshmallows or whipped cream. I drank about half of it and dumped the rest down the sink, then I went back to the library.

Jonathan was still on the phone. "Nothing's come up, I promise. I was just curious." He rolled his eyes at me. "I took a couple days off. I'm staying with a friend. ... I already gave you the phone number. ... Just a minute. What's the address here?"

"My address? It's two twenty Mariposa Lane."

He repeated it into the phone. "I have to go, Mom ... There's no reason for you to do that. Nothing's going on, I— Yeah, okay, talk to you later."

He hung up and said to me, "Horst Martinez made the peace symbol. He gave it to my father. She said he always wore it. He was wearing it when he left for work the last time." He ran a hand through his hair and sighed. "She's cutting her vacation short and coming home. She thinks my father's been spotted."

"Oh ... I'm sorry, Jonathan. Is she going to be really upset when she finds out he's dead?"

"She hates him."

"But that's because she thinks he ran out on her. He didn't."

"So where's he been for twenty-seven years?"

I wanted to stamp my foot and yell at him because I was getting tired of him not believing me, but he looked so sad I just sighed and said, "In my backyard, Jonathan."

Chapter Sixteen

Jonathan was waiting for someone to call him back with Horst Martinez's address, so I took a shower and got dressed. I already had an idea how I was going to approach Martinez so I dressed up: the intimidate-them-with-wealth theory again. I chose a crinkly cotton dress in a pale cream color that looked sort of like a loose-fitting slip—thin straps, a scoop neck, just a hint of a waist. The bottom of the calf-length skirt was a zig-zagging strip of pale cream cotton lace. I put on the matching short-sleeved jacket, which was also loose-fitting with a nar-rower band of zig-zaggy lace around the bottom, and cream-colored sandals with two-inch heels and a matching shoulder bag in soft leather. Then I added a little color—gold, to be precise. Gold heart-shaped earrings, a gold chain made of hearts linked together around my neck, a matching bracelet, and a gold ring on each hand. I twirled around and asked Charlie what he thought.

"*Pretty.*"

"I was shooting for stinking rich."

"*Pretty and stinking rich.*"

I smiled and took one more look in the mirror. I did look pretty good.

Jonathan was dressed. His hair was still wet from the shower and he was wearing stone-washed jeans and a light-blue T-shirt and dark blue Nikes. "Wow," he said when he saw me. "Where are you going?"

"To see Horst Martinez, I hope. Did you get his address?"

"Yeah, and his phone number, but he isn't there. He's at Oak Valley College. They're working on the display the rest of the week and he's there to be sure they get it right. Sounds like the temperamental-artist type to me. Did you have breakfast?"

"Just some cocoa."

"You need to buy groceries."

"Well, I'm not dressed for the supermarket right now. We can eat out if you want. There's a place right by the campus called the Morning Sun Café. They have all kinds of yummy things."

I got *The Art Of Horst Martinez* from the library and we went outside. Jonathan said we should take the Porsche because I was overdressed for his Chevy. I walked around to the driver's side.

"Lizbet?"

I looked across the roof of the car at Jonathan, who was standing by the passenger door. "What?"

"Look, I don't have any hang-ups about women drivers. Suzanne—my partner—she drives more often than I do and she's a hell of a good cop, too. It isn't that you're a woman, it's just ..."

"What? I'm a good driver."

He grinned at me, Charlie's little-boy grin. "I've never driven a Porsche."

I tossed the keys to him and walked around to the passenger side. I opened the door, then stood there and fiddled with the strap of my purse to give Charlie time to get into what passes for a back seat in the Porsche. I think his knees were probably poking into the back of my seat, but since I couldn't feel them, I didn't let it bother me. We were halfway down Foothill Avenue when Jonathan asked if my answering machine was turned on. "Braverman's supposed to call this morning."

"Oh, yeah, I forgot. The machine's always on. It has remote message retrieval or whatever you call it. We can call after a bit and see if he left a message. I wonder what Sterling's doing. He must have given up on following me."

"I think he hired someone to do it for him."

"What?"

"You see that dark blue Ford, three cars back?"

I turned around to look out the rear window. "Uh-huh."

"I recognized the driver. He's a retired San Jose cop named Bill Colton. He has a private investigator's license. Does security work mostly."

"You're kidding! Isn't there some law against Sterling having people spy on me?"

"Harassment, maybe. You want me to stop by the police department so you can report it?"

I didn't bother answering. I spent the rest of the drive wondering what Suzanne the Wonder Cop looked like.

We found a parking place near the campus, then walked to the Morning Sun Café. I had Belgian waffles with blueberries. Jonathan ordered a mushroom omelet. Charlie had some of each. I also had hot chocolate, which came with a long piece of stick cinnamon and a huge mound of whipped cream. I asked Jonathan if he knew how to hire a cook.

"Put an ad in the paper, I guess. Maybe one of your neighbors could recommend someone."

"I don't really know any of them."

"They probably think you're a real snobby bitch. Why don't you just go knock on some doors and introduce yourself?"

"I don't know if rich people do things like that."

Jonathan shook his head, like he couldn't believe anyone could be so stupid. "Maybe there's a class you could take. 'Coping With Instant Wealth' or something like that."

"Don't make fun of me."

"If I suddenly got rich, I sure as hell wouldn't waste my time worrying about what a bunch of other rich people thought of me."

"What would you do?"

"Have fun. Buy a Porsche. Travel. Chase rich blonde babes." He finished off the last of his omelet and checked out my plate. "You going to eat the rest of that?"

The waffle was wonderful, but I'd only eaten half of it and I was stuffed. I handed the plate to him. "It isn't as easy as it sounds. You'd meet some gorgeous woman and fall head over heals in love with her and then she'd dump you when she found out you don't know which fork to use."

Jonathan swallowed a huge bite of Belgian waffle. "Hey, I'm not as low-class as I look. I know all about salad forks and dessert forks and shrimp cocktail forks and how to sniff the wine cork and swish a little around in my mouth and tell the *sommelier* I'd prefer the Chateau Chapeau Chartreuse 'eighty-two."

"Tell the who?"

"The wine guy in a restaurant. You just need to get a good etiquette book."

What I really need is a whole different childhood. But maybe a book would help.

Jonathan finally finished eating everything in sight and we walked to the campus, which is real pretty and even though it's right smack dab in the middle of downtown, you feel like you're out in the country. All the buildings are red brick and there are lots of big trees and fountains and statues and some sculptures that look like a giant's child left broken toys lying around.

The sculpture in front of the Art Center was huge. It was really nothing but two big pipes, painted flat black and twisted at funny angles. "Look, Ch—I mean, Jonathan. It's one of Horst Martinez's things." I read the name on a brass plaque stuck in the ground. It was called "Utopia." Don't ask me why.

Jonathan had given me a sharp look when I almost called him Charlie. I sure hoped he didn't have his heart set on finding his father alive. He didn't really seem to care if Charlie was dead or alive, but you never can tell with men.

He suddenly leaned close to me and whispered, "Don't look around, but Bill Colton's lurking behind a tree."

"Damn! Sterling makes me so mad. You'd think this was Russia or something. I have a perfect right to go where I want without a private eye following me."

Jonathan wasn't real interested in whether or not some cop was violating my rights. I wasn't surprised. He was a cop, too. He probably spent whole days violating people's rights.

I had explained my plan to him while we were eating. He wasn't happy with it, since it meant he didn't get to tag along, but Charlie thought it might work. We went inside the Art Center. The lobby had big abstract paintings on the walls and four maroon sofas arranged in a square in the middle, so each one faced a wall. The space formed by the backs of the sofas was full of plants. Jonathan sat on the sofa that faced the entrance and I went to the information desk.

The woman who was sitting on the corner of it was a college-girl type, with long frizzy brown hair and gold-rimmed glasses and skin the color of coffee with cream. I couldn't decide what ethnic group she belonged to. She was very thin and was wearing a brown suede skirt that was mid-calf length, brown suede boots, and a brown baggy shirt with big bright orange flowers on it. She told me the Horst Martinez exhibit didn't open until Friday afternoon.

"I know. I'm here to see Mr. Martinez."

She twirled a long strand of frizzy hair around her finger while she checked out my jewelry, then she shrugged and said, "Upstairs. Second door on the right."

The stairs were wide and curving. The second door on the right led to a big room with four gray couches in the center and plants in the space behind them. I guess that's so you can sit down and admire the art on the walls. A sign on a tall easel by the door said WALL ART BY HORST MARTINEZ.

There were eight or ten people in the room. Most of them were opening wooden crates. Across the room, a woman in a yellow T-shirt and an extremely short blue denim skirt was on a stepladder, straightening a wall-hanging made of thick rope and brass rings. Horst Martinez was steadying the ladder for her. He looked just like his picture, with maybe just a little more gray in his hair. He was wearing a blue T-shirt and white bib overalls like house painters wear. He kept glancing upward and the thought crossed my mind that he had quite a view, but I thought, no, that was just my dirty mind. He was a famous artist, after all.

Then he spotted me and I knew right away that he really was looking up that girl's skirt. I can spot a lech a mile away. He watched me walk toward him like he was trying to picture me bending over in front of him wearing split-crotch panties and shoes with four-inch heels. If I'd had a shoe like that handy, I'd have jabbed the heel into a strategic part of his anatomy.

He forgot all about steadying the ladder and hurried toward me, his hand already held out. From the look in his eyes I knew he really wanted to grab my breast but there were too many people around so he settled for taking my hand, holding onto it instead of just shaking it. "Have we met?" he asked. "Surely I wouldn't forget you." He didn't have an accent at all, not German or Spanish, just plain old Californian.

"No, we haven't. My name's Elizabeth Dutton."

He didn't bother telling me his name. He probably thought everyone in the entire world knew who he was.

"The display doesn't officially open until Friday," he said, sliding his hand up my arm and caressing the inside of my elbow, "but if you'd like a private tour ..."

"I'm interested in buying something."

"Ah. And you'd be a worthy owner. Perhaps we could have lunch and afterward I can show you which pieces are available. They should have most of it unpacked by then."

"I just had breakfast."

"A bit later, I meant. Until then, there's a small conference room available. Some coffee, perhaps? You can tell me what type of piece you're interested in."

I knew exactly what type of piece *he* was interested in. I moved back a little, so his hand slid off my arm. "It's a particular pendant you made." I opened the *Art of Horst Martinez.*

"A pendant? I'm sorry, I haven't made jewelry in years. There are pieces in private collections, but I don't—"

"This one," I said, and showed him the picture on page thirty-seven.

He stared at the picture.

"You see," I said, "my parents were hippies back in the 'sixties and they had an old silver peace symbol, not real silver like this one, just a cheap thing, but it was very important to them. It's ruined though, and they died a few years ago and I want to buy the pendant and donate it to a museum and have a little sign by it that says 'in memory of' and their names."

I had practiced exactly what I was going to say and I don't think he even heard me. He finally stopped looking at the picture, but his eyes never met mine again. He looked past me at the wall or whatever was back there.

"I'm sorry, I don't make jewelry anymore. That piece—I don't even know where it is now. I haven't seen it in years and years."

"This picture was taken in nineteen eighty-eight."

"Well, that's years ago, isn't it?" he snapped. "I'm sorry, I don't do jewelry anymore. If you'll excuse me, there's a lot of work to be done."

He walked away quickly, but instead of going back to work, he left the room. I was trying to decide what to do when I saw Jonathan walk past the open door, following Martinez. I peeked into the hall. Jonathan was standing with his back flattened against the wall right next to an open door. He motioned for me to go away. I went downstairs. I sat on one of the maroon couches. Bill Colton, Sterling's spy, was hiding behind a newspaper on another couch.

"That was pretty weird, wasn't it, Charlie? He didn't even want to talk about your peace symbol."

Charlie was smiling, looking pretty pleased actually. *"Horst Martinez and Samuel Towne. And I never even suspected."*

"You really think he was mixed up in it?"

"Had to be. Did you see his face when you showed him the pendant? You scared the shit out of him. If he didn't know I was murdered, he wouldn't have any reason to worry about someone taking an interest in the pendant. He'd probably have a long-winded

story about how he happened to get it back after the cop he gave it to disappeared."

"That picture ... it wasn't posed, was it? I bet he didn't mean to be photographed wearing the peace symbol. Could they put it in the book without his permission?"

"Sure, all the publisher would need is the photographer's permission. I doubt that Martinez had anything to do with the book, other than being interviewed by the author. He probably didn't know that picture was going to be in it until it was too late to do anything about it."

"This is getting a little scary, Charlie. Do you think he's the one who attacked Betty Yakamoto?"

"He doesn't look like the type to do his own dirty work. Sterling opened his big mouth to someone in the police department."

"Jeez, Charlie, you're scaring me. If there's a cop out there trying to be sure no one finds out he had something to do with blowing up that building and killing those cops and killing you—well, I really don't want to run into him."

"At least you've got Jonathan on your side."

"He doesn't even believe me."

"Here he comes." I turned my head and saw Jonathan coming down the stairs. He gave his head a little jerk toward the door, so I followed him outside. He was crouched down right outside the door, tying his shoe. Without looking up, he said, "Meet me at the car."

"I think he believes you now," Charlie said.

Chapter Seventeen

Charlie and I were in the car for about five minutes before Jonathan showed up. I was in the driver's seat because the way he had acted, I thought maybe we were going to be trying to get away from someone. When he finally showed up, he opened my door and said, "Let me drive, okay?" I moved into the passenger seat, which involved wriggling over the gear shift and wasn't very dignified at all. Jonathan slid into his seat, brushed his hair back off his forehead, laughed, and then said, "Holy shit, Lizbet. What have you gotten us into?"

"What did Martinez do?"

He put his seatbelt on and said, "Let's go someplace where we can talk. I want to lose Colton for a while, too." He started the engine and pulled out of the parking place.

"What was the double-oh-seven act back there all about? I thought maybe someone was after you."

"I just wanted to see which of us Colton is more interested in. He followed you."

Jonathan didn't know his way around Oak Valley very well and I don't really drive around downtown much, so we managed to get lost, but that was okay because we managed to lose Sterling's spy, too. The last I saw of Colton, he was sitting at a red light watching the Porsche head the wrong way on a one-way street. Jonathan honked right back at three or four drivers who blew their horns at him, then he made a quick turn into a parking lot and drove straight through it to the exit, ignoring the attendant completely, and turned onto the street that was a block behind the corner where I'd last seen Colton's car. Jonathan headed in the opposite direction, made three or four quick turns, found a street I recognized, and then we headed for the freeway.

"How about my place?" he said.

If I had a dollar for every time a guy's said that to me, I wouldn't need Tom's money. "Fine," I said.

We didn't talk at all during the drive. The windows were down and the wind blowing through the car would have made it hard to carry on a conversation anyway. Jonathan seemed really hyped-up, drumming his fingers on the steering wheel and driving fast, whipping the car around curves and coasting through stop signs. I guess if you have a badge in your pocket, you don't worry about tickets.

He lived on the south side of San Jose in an expensive-looking apartment complex that was white stucco with a Spanish-style red tile roof. Small balconies jutted out from the second floor. It was the kind of place I dreamed of having before Tom died.

I thought there was probably room for two large bedrooms and a bathroom upstairs, but I didn't ask. The small living room was furnished very plainly, just a couch and two matching chairs in a dark blue print, a coffee table, two end tables with lamps on them, and nothing on the wall but a big painting of a ship on a stormy sea over the couch. Jonathan walked through the living room like it wasn't a place he ever stopped.

The other room was a lot more interesting. It was a

combination family room and dining room and was separated from the kitchen by a counter. The furniture looked old and comfortable and none of it really matched any other piece. One wall was taken up with shelves made from stained boards and glass blocks. Some of the shelves were full of books, others held stacks of CDs and tapes, others apparently were for whatever Jonathan happened to have in his hand when he walked by. There were some wrist and ankle weights, a baseball mitt, stacks of mail, a jar of coins, a gun that was in two or three pieces, a shoebox half full of photographs, two cameras, a couple sweatshirts, and all kinds of other things I didn't really have time to look at.

Jonathan almost shoved me into a chair—not rudely, just like he was in a hurry to get down to business—and said, "How did you know that was my father's body in your backyard?"

Things were not off to a good start. That was the one question I couldn't answer. Charlie gave me a reassuring little smile. "I can't tell you. I just know. How come you all of a sudden believe it's true?"

Jonathan walked over to the counter, turned one of the tall stools so it was facing me, and sat down. "All right. We play it your way. Martinez made a phone call. He said—word for word, okay? But all I heard was his side of the conversation. First he said, 'What the fuck's going on? Some broad's here asking about Bilbo's goddam peace symbol.' Then he said, 'Cute little thing, real classy, born-with-a-silver-spoon-in-her-mouth type, reddish hair.' Then he said, 'I didn't catch her name. Yeah, Elizabeth something.'"

"He really said that?"

"Yeah, Bilbo's goddam peace symbol. His words exactly."

"I meant about me being classy."

"For Chr—Yes, he really said that."

"Then what?"

"Then he said, 'How the hell would I know?' and then he didn't say anything for a minute then he said, 'You better make sure of it,' then he said, 'She saw it in the damn book. I'd like to wring that photographer's neck, sneaking up on me like that and then swearing he wouldn't print it. I knew when I saw it in the book there was going to be trouble someday.' Then he and whoever he was talking to seemed to be arguing about whose fault it was that the photograph ended up in the book. Martinez kept saying he didn't even see it until it was already in the stores. Then he said, 'She had to get a permit to put the fucking pool in. You should've kept an eye on things like that.' Then he said, 'You better make damn sure of it,' and he slammed the phone down and I got the hell out of there."

"So ... it really sounds like he knew it was Charlie's body, doesn't it?"

"Sure does. I wish I knew who he was talking to."

"A cop, I bet. A cop has to be mixed up in it."

"Could be. If that was Charlie's body, it had to be buried the night of the explosion. The grass was put down the next morning, right? and the Altmans moved in. Check your answering machine. Maybe Braverman will have something for us."

I didn't have any messages, though, so Jonathan called Braverman's Landscaping. He made some notes on a pad of paper, said thanks and hung up, looking a little stunned.

"What is it?"

"Do you know who the Chief of Police of Oak Valley is?"

"Um ... well, he's in the paper all the time. Martin or something like that."

"Miller. Winston Miller."

"Well, why'd you ask if you already knew?"

"He's retiring. The Deputy Chief of Police is in line for his job and Sterling's hoping to step into the Deputy Chief spot."

"Yeah, so?"

"Jacob Braverman hired three men to work on your lawn. His oldest son supervised them. Two of them were college kids who'd worked for him the previous summer. The third one also worked for him summers when he was in college, but he graduated the year before and had a full-time job. Whenever he was assigned to swing shift or night shift, he'd give Braverman a call and let him know he was available so he could pick up some extra money."

"He was a cop, right? Moonlighting—or is it daylighting if you do it in the daytime? What was his name?"

"Theodore Van Horne."

"Is he still a cop?"

"Yeah, he's a cop, all right. He's Deputy Chief. He's the guy Sterling hopes to replace. He's the man who's going to be Chief of Police of Oak Valley in a few months."

Chapter Eighteen

"Maybe we should tell Captain Sterling."

Jonathan was shoving clothes into the washing machine, which was in a small laundry room at the back of the kitchen. After dropping Braverman's little bombshell, he suddenly decided he should do some laundry since he was home. I think he just needed to do something because he was so keyed up. He dumped the contents of a laundry basket in the washer. It was mostly underwear but there were also a couple pairs of jeans and a bright red, new-looking sweatshirt. He dumped detergent straight out of the box into the machine without measuring it, then let the lid of the washer clang shut and said, "What?"

"What about telling Sterling?"

"How do we know for sure he's not involved? I don't think he is, but he already thinks we're in cahoots and doesn't trust either one of us. I don't have any proof Martinez's phone call ever took place and we can't even prove the bones are Charlie's. The only thing we might be able to prove is that Horst Martinez was photographed in nineteen eighty-eight wearing a peace symbol that belonged to Charlie Bilbo in nineteen sixty-nine. And what does that prove?"

"Nothing, I guess."

"Are you hungry? I'm starving."

"Jonathan, we just ate." He didn't pay any attention. I followed him into the kitchen. He peered into the refrigerator, which was nearly empty, then opened a couple cupboard doors, sighed, and made a peanut butter sandwich, which he ate in about three bites.

One time, when I was still in school and living at home, Lady said something about how Duke would starve to death if she wasn't around to cook for him. Then she got a funny look on her face and said, "My god, when did I turn into my mother?" I think that's why I dropped out of school and ran away from home. I didn't ever want to wonder when I turned into *my* mother. So I ended up serving chili dogs to truck drivers.

Watching Jonathan screw up a load of laundry and scrape enough peanut butter for a sandwich out of an almost-empty jar gave me this tremendous urge to tell him to go watch a ball game while I did his damn laundry and fixed him something to eat. Lady was right. She always used to tell me that women are biologically trapped because they're ruled by the maternal instinct. Lady was pretty deep sometimes. Men, I happen to know for a fact, are ruled by the I-gotta-get-laid instinct.

"What about Theodore Van Horne working on my lawn? That isn't proof, I guess, but it sure is suspicious. He was right there where Charlie was buried."

"But we can't prove it was Charlie and no one can pinpoint exactly when the body was buried."

"What about telling the San Jose cops? They'd believe you, wouldn't they?"

"Maybe, but what can they do without some kind of evidence? Plus, it's out of their jurisdiction."

"Well, we have to do *something.*"

"We have to get some evidence."

"Your mother could swear that Charlie was wearing the pendant the night he died."

"She could swear he had it on when he left the house, but it was twenty-seven years ago and anyone could question her memory. And all Martinez would have to do is claim he ran into Charlie and got it back. Maybe a stone was loose and Charlie asked him to fix it or something and when Charlie disappeared he just kept it. He could even use that as an excuse for being upset when you asked about it, say he always felt bad that he didn't return it to my mother."

"Well, phooey. What about the FBI?"

"They'd just screw it up. Lizbet, you have to tell me what else you know. How'd you know it was Charlie's body? How do you know the dental x-rays were switched?"

"I can't—"

"Dammit! I'm tired of this stupid game. Don't you see you could be in danger? Sterling may be a captain, but he still has to account for his time. He had to tell someone what he was working on and I think he told Van Horne. He probably told him how hard it was to get Betty Yakamoto's name and before he had time to talk to her, Van Horne broke into her house looking for the x-rays. Pretty soon he's going to realize the x-rays aren't any danger to him as long as you're not running around telling people about them."

"You mean he'd—"

"Kill you? Why not? You act like you've got some kind of proof that Charlie Bilbo was murdered and if you're right, Van Horne's got a whole lot to lose if anyone finds out."

"I don't have any proof."

"Then how—"

"I can't explain it. I just—I just put two and two together."

"*Christ.* Next you're going to tell me it was women's intuition."

"It was something like that, actually." We went round and round for a long time, with him insisting that I had to tell him everything I knew and me insisting that I couldn't. We ended up yelling, like we'd known each other for years instead of twenty-four hours.

Jonathan eventually stalked off to put his clothes in the dryer. I heard him mutter "Son of a *bitch!*" and smiled to myself. I thought he'd look kind of cute in pink underwear.

I went into the living room where it was quiet and dark because the drapes were closed. *"This is a big mess, Charlie. How are we ever going to prove what happened? It was too long ago."* Charlie just shrugged. I sat on the couch, thinking that it would be nice if I knew *why* I was getting all mixed up in something I didn't even understand. *"Are we supposed to clear your name, Charlie? Is that it?"*

"I don't think that's possible, Lizbet."

"Why not?"

He shrugged again. *"Like you said, it was too long ago."*

"So what's the point of all this? You said there had to be a reason."

"We're supposed to change something, keep something from happening. Maybe it's Van Horne we're supposed to stop. If he was involved in my murder—and it sure seems like he must have at least suggested a place to dump my body—he can't have many scruples, which makes him a pretty poor choice for a chief of police. When I died, things that were supposed to happen didn't. Maybe if the bust had gone down the way it was supposed to, Van Horne's involvement would have come to light and then he never would have gotten where he is today."

"So we're supposed to change the future."

"In a way."

"I don't know, Charlie. Being the chief of police in Oak Valley isn't that big a deal."

"It puts him in a position of power. Maybe he has contacts with people who know how to use his power for their own purposes. Maybe he'll be chief of police for a while, then he'll go into politics, run for governor or something like that. Police chief could just be the first step. It could be something way down the road that has to be stopped."

"Well, if whoever's in charge where you come from knows all that, why doesn't he—or she or it or whatever—just give Van Horne a major coronary?"

He smiled and said, *"No one—nothing—controls the future. People have free will, Lizbet, nothing is pre-ordained."*

I couldn't decide whether that was comforting or not. It's kind of nice to think that everything is already planned out, so when I do something totally stupid it isn't really my fault. It's just the way it was meant to be. Free will sounds scary to me. That means I'm responsible for my own life and if there's anyone I wouldn't want to trust with my life, it's me.

Jonathan walked into the room, saying, "Why are you sitting in the dark?" He opened the drapes, then sat down next to me on the couch and took my hand in his. "Listen, I've been thinking. There's no way we can ever reconstruct what happened that night, let alone come up with proof. What we need to do is figure out who the weak link is and make him talk."

"Martinez or Van Horne, you mean? Make one of them rat on the other? How?"

Jonathan had a plan, which I didn't like one bit. He wanted me to go to Van Horne, tell him I was concerned that the police weren't properly investigating the body in my backyard, and tell him I had proof that the bones were Charlie Bilbo's. I was supposed to be evasive then, and tell him I couldn't get the proof until the next day. And then we would sit around waiting to see what happened. What Jonathan thought would happen was that Van Horne would come after me. I removed my hand from his.

"I get it. Since we can't prove who murdered Charlie, you'll get Van Horne arrested for murdering me."

"I wasn't planning on you getting murdered."

"No? Sure sounded like it to me. I don't think so, Jonathan. I don't want to get anywhere near Van Horne or that creep Martinez."

"You wouldn't be in danger, Lizbet, I'd be right there."

"Oh, yeah? Well, how about this: We tell Sterling your mother was the other woman in the dentist's office and he'll tell Van Horne about it and then Van Horne will go after your mother. Instead of me."

Jonathan took a deep breath, let it out slowly, and actually had the good grace to look a little embarrassed. "All right, you've made your point. We'll come up with another plan."

We didn't have time though because the doorbell rang and it was Jonathan's mother. Amanda Dillon Bilbo Reynolds wasn't just a tiny bit plump anymore. She looked a lot like Shelley Winters in the *Poseidon Adventure*. Charlie didn't look at all surprised, but then he hadn't been surprised to see Jonathan either and he'd changed even more than Amanda had since that picture was taken in the backyard the day before he died.

"How'd you get here so fast?" Jonathan asked.

"I flew. Martha and Karen are staying and they'll drive the Winnebago back. There wasn't any point in ruining their vacation, too. What's going on, Jonathan?"

Jonathan suddenly remembered I existed and introduced us. His mother didn't seem overjoyed to meet me. She looked at me like I was a glob of snot on the wall.

"Nothing's going on," Jonathan said.

Amanda crossed her arms. "Don't you lie to me. Your father's been spotted, hasn't he?"

"No. Actually ..."

"What?"

"I think there's a good chance he died the night of the explosion."

Amanda turned white. Jonathan grabbed her arm and steered her into a chair. "What are you saying?" she asked, her voice weak and squeaky.

"I'm sorry, I shouldn't have sprung it on you like that. A skeleton turned up in Lizbet's backyard. I think it might be his."

"What are you *saying?* He's been dead all these years? How? That can't be true. He took the money, he—he left me." She started crying.

"Mom, I'm sorry. I don't know for sure, but—"

The doorbell rang again. As Jonathan went to the door, Amanda got up and hurried into the other room, sniffling loudly. Sterling was his usual charming self. He sat down without being asked and said, "Mrs. Yakamoto called my office and left a message. She remembered the name of the other woman who worked in McMillan's office. Mandy Reynolds. I haven't got a line on her yet."

There was a very peculiar silence. Jonathan glanced toward the doorway to the room where his mother was still sniffling softly. Sterling hadn't spoken in a quiet voice. Amanda had to have heard her name mentioned. But nobody did anything. I knew she was Mandy Reynolds and Jonathan knew she was Mandy Reynolds and *she* certainly knew she was Mandy Reynolds and none of us said a word. Jonathan met my eyes very briefly then looked away.

Sterling just sat there and looked at us. I had the feeling

we both looked guilty. Jonathan eventually cleared his throat and said, "How about calling Colton off."

"Huh?" Sterling said.

Jonathan gave him a long look. "Bill Colton. Call him off. There's no reason for him to follow Lizbet all over. He's not any good at it anyway. It took me all of five minutes to lose him."

"What the hell are you talking about?"

"Are you saying you didn't hire him?"

"Are you talking about the Bill Colton that used to be a cop, does investigations now? No, I didn't hire him. Why would I hire him?"

"Somebody must have hired him. He followed Lizbet downtown from her house this morning and he hung around until I decided to lose him."

Sterling was looking a little shocked. "Are you sure?"

"Sure I'm sure. He's driving an 'eighty-nine Ford, dark blue."

Sterling puzzled over that for a moment. I decided to help him out. "If you didn't ask him to follow me, then whoever you blabbed to did."

"She's right, Sterling. You told someone you were looking for the dental records. He searched Betty Yakamoto's house and now he's having Lizbet tailed."

"I didn't tell anyone outside the department. I got better sense than that."

"Give that some thought, Sterling. Give it some long hard thought." Jonathan was smiling but not the way he smiled at me. A cop smile. Definitely a cop smile.

Sterling stood up. "Are you saying ..?"

"I'm saying you should ask your pal where he was the night the SAMIC headquarters was bombed."

"You're crazy."

"Ask him. In the meantime, are you here for some good

reason or did you just want to prove you can find Lizbet wherever she goes?"

"Just wanted to let you know I'm still looking for the x-rays. Wouldn't want Ms. Lange thinking I'm not taking her seriously."

"Bullshit, Sterling. You're harassing her and you know it and I know it."

"I also wanted to let you know I got the other woman's name. I'm going to be keeping a close watch out. Anything happens to a woman named Mandy Reynolds anywhere in the state, I'll be on you two like mean on a junkyard dog."

There was another of those peculiar silences. I heard a slight movement in the other room. Amanda wasn't very far away. She couldn't help but hear everything Sterling said.

"See you around," Sterling said and got up and walked to the door. He gave us a long hard look before he left.

I looked at Jonathan. "He's going to find out about your mother and then he's really going to be mad at us."

Amanda came into the room, a wad of tissue in one hand. Her eyes were red and puffy. "Who was that awful man?"

"He's an Oak Valley cop. He's trying to find Dad's old dental records."

"I already told you they're gone."

"I know."

A really bright idea popped into my mind so suddenly I almost looked up to see if a lightbulb had appeared over my head. "Hey," I said, "he was your husband! You'd know about his teeth! Jonathan, she needs to tell Sterling that Charlie was missing two teeth and had a permanent bridge. Then he'll know for sure those x-rays were switched."

Amanda looked at me coldly. "What are you talking about? Charlie had almost perfect teeth. He had two or three small fillings, that's all."

Chapter Nineteen

I suddenly announced I had to go to the bathroom because I was afraid if I "talked" to Charlie it would be obvious I was really upset. Jonathan said, "To the left at the top of the stairs." The bathroom was blue and white and cleaner than I expected. Most men's bathrooms I've seen have left a little something to be desired as far as sanitation goes, but Jonathan's looked like he cleaned it on a regular basis. I hadn't really needed to go, but of course as soon as I got in the room I did, so I told Charlie to go away.

He came back while I was washing my hands. He either had awfully good timing or he didn't go nearly as far away as I wanted him to while I was doing things I consider private. *"Well, Charlie?"*

He opened his mouth wide and used his little finger to pull back his lip on the left side. Even from four feet away, I could see the gold surfaces of two top molars.

"Do you think she just forgot? Maybe she mixed you up with her second husband."

"Remember the x-rays you saw in Sterling's office?"

"Yeah. Very good teeth. Only three fillings. But, Charlie, that means ... What does it mean? She's deliberately lying? That means she

knows the x-rays the cops have aren't yours. She's known it all these years. But why, Charlie?"

"It would be interesting to find out, wouldn't it?" Charlie smiled, a cop smile. Like father, like son. Ghosts apparently aren't very sentimental about the things they leave behind. Like wives.

We went back downstairs. Jonathan had explained about Sterling's search for the dental records and the attack on Betty Yakamoto. Amanda was pretty shook up. Jonathan didn't have to ask her twice to stay at his place. She'd taken a taxi home from the airport and had called my house from her apartment. When she didn't get an answer there, she drove to Jonathan's apartment.

Jonathan said he'd go get her suitcase, which she'd left in her living room. He had his own car keys out before he remembered his car was at my house. Amanda was going to give him the keys to her car, but I jumped right in and said I'd take him. Charlie gave me a thumbs up. I didn't see what my going to Amanda's apartment would accomplish. I just didn't want to be left alone with her. She was still looking at me like I was something nice people don't talk about.

It was about a five-mile drive. On the way, Jonathan apologized for his mother's reaction to me. "She thinks every woman I meet is going to be just like my ex-wife."

"You've been married?"

"Hasn't everyone? It was back when I was young and foolish."

"Do you have any kids?"

"I said foolish, not stupid. Did my mother blow your theory about the x-rays being switched?"

"I think she's confused."

"You're persistent, aren't you? Well, it was a long time ago. Maybe she doesn't remember."

Or maybe she's lying. But I kept that thought to myself. Trying to fit Amanda into the Martinez/Van Horne/Towne/ SAMIC equation made my head ache.

Amanda lived on the second floor of a building in a complex of at least fifteen identical apartment buildings. Her apartment wasn't nearly as nice as Jonathan's. It was decorated in Early American, heavy on the browns and oranges. The living room looked like one of those display rooms in furniture stores, with everything matching and arranged just so. Jonathan said he wanted to check for signs of a break-in, so he headed toward the back of the apartment.

"Look," Charlie said. He was pointing at the wall by the front door. A wooden thing that was made to look like a big brass padlock was hanging there. There were three hooks on it, a key dangling from each one. Two of them looked like car keys. I took the other one and slipped it into my purse. Don't ask me why. It just seemed like the thing to do.

"Everything looks fine," Jonathan said, picking up Amanda's suitcase. "Let's go."

He didn't have to ask me twice. I'd just stolen something for the first time in my life. Well, if you don't count that lipstick I shoplifted when I was thirteen. All of a sudden I understood why criminals are always in a rush to get away from the scene of the crime. I felt like the *furniture* was pointing its finger at me.

On the way back to Jonathan's apartment, I told him I wanted to go home. Naturally we had a big argument about that. I kept telling him about the alarm system and he kept saying I could still be in danger. He also slipped up and let me know he still didn't trust me and wasn't about to let me out of his sight. When I said he could stay at my house again, he pointed out that his mother would be alone at his apartment and she was probably in more danger than I was. I was so mad by that time I had to bite the inside of my cheeks to keep from telling him his mother was a liar and knew damn well the cops had the wrong x-rays. Then I felt so bad thinking how upset he'd be when he did find out that I said his mother could stay at my house, too. Which is how Amanda ended up following us up to the Foothills.

I checked the backyard as soon as we got in the house. We'd left so early no cops had been there but they must have come later. The crime scene ribbon was gone. I showed Amanda to the bedroom next to Jonathan's room, which has white furniture and is all decorated in pale green. She seemed a little overwhelmed by the house and didn't have much to say. She'd probably been thinking that I blew all my tips on expensive clothes so I could trap some innocent man like her precious son.

Charlie said, *"Now all we have to do is wait until they go to bed tonight."*

I gave him a suspicious look. *"What does that mean?"*

"So you can go search Amanda's apartment."

Somehow I knew that was coming. "Oh, shit."

"What's wrong?" Jonathan had just come downstairs after carrying his mother's suitcase to her room.

"Nothing."

"Chip another nail? I'll go to the grocery store with you if you want."

"Don't you ever think about anything but food?"

He grinned. "Sure. But food's high on my list of priorities."

I went upstairs and changed clothes, putting on jeans and a pink top and white Reeboks with pink laces. I dumped all my stuff in a denim shoulder bag with a design in tiny pink beads on the front. Amanda didn't seem worried about staying alone after I explained the alarm system and showed her where the panic buttons were. I think she was dying to snoop around anyway.

We spent over an hour in the store and left with six bags full. I kept telling Jonathan that I didn't cook much and he said if I was going to interview cooks I should have some food in the kitchen so they wouldn't think I was too cheap to buy groceries. I told him I wasn't really serious about hiring a cook and he said I was an idiot to eat take-out junk food instead of hiring a good cook and did it ever occur to me that I was depriving someone of a job? Actually, I hadn't ever thought about it that way.

It was four o'clock when we got back to the house. It took almost an hour to get the groceries put away and the pantry organized to Jonathan's satisfaction. You'd have thought he was planning to move in.

Amanda was in the casual living room, watching the big-screen TV. She had my bag of pretzels and a Coke and said she hoped I didn't mind her making herself at home. I said "Not at all." I lie real good.

Jonathan and I talked for a while but neither of us could come up with any good ideas, so eventually we ended up in three different rooms watching three different TVs. Just like family. After buying all that food, nobody cooked dinner. We all made sandwiches and sat in front of our televisions eating them. Since Amanda seemed to feel the big screen was hers and Jonathan was downstairs in the rec room where he could watch a basketball game and work out at the same time, I was in the formal living room. I hadn't even known there was a television in there until I opened a door on the fancy built-in wall unit a couple weeks after I moved in.

At ten o'clock I took a shower, got dressed, and stretched out on my bed. The television was on but I was too nervous to notice what was on. I was wearing black jeans and black socks and a black T-shirt under a blue velour caftan. Jonathan came looking for me at about eleven and told me Amanda was already in bed and he was going to turn in. He stood in the doorway for a minute, like maybe he thought I was going to invite him to join me. "See you in the morning," he finally said and shut my door for me.

As soon as I heard his door close, I got up and pulled off the caftan, then put on a pair of black sneakers and a black hooded sweatshirt. I stuck Amanda's key and my driver's license in my jeans pocket along with eighty dollars in cash, put my own keys in the sweatshirt pocket, turned off the television and the lights and the switch to the alarm on the door to the balcony. I went outside and crept down the stairway to the patio. A few seconds later, I was behind the garage, unlocking the door that goes into a storage room that has an inside door to the garage itself. *"What if he hears the car, Charlie?"*

"You'll be halfway down the hill before he gets his pants on. How noisy is the door?"

"It's automatic. I don't know if you can hear it in the house or not. He's way at the other end. Maybe he won't hear it."

Jonathan had driven the Porsche into the garage so he'd seen the other cars. I was tempted to take my old Nova, but I hadn't driven it since the day I moved in and I was afraid it might not start after sitting for so long. I decided to use the Volvo. At least it was a little less conspicuous than the Porsche. I hit the button on the remote for the garage door and as soon as it started moving I turned the key in the ignition. My heart was pounding and I felt sick to my stomach. I expected Jonathan to show up any second. When the door was high enough, I drove the Volvo out of the garage, leaving the headlights off. I stopped in the driveway just long enough to use the remote again to lower the door. No lights came on in the house.

We were halfway down Foothill Avenue before my heartbeat slowed down to normal.

Chapter Twenty

Charlie and I both kept watching for headlights behind us all the way down the hill. Sterling and Colton had either given up following me around or they'd fallen asleep and hadn't seen me leave. It took over an hour to get to Amanda's apartment building, mainly because I couldn't remember exactly where it was.

The first thing that went wrong is that there was a light on in Amanda's living room. "Maybe she has a roommate, Charlie. I didn't think about asking. She could be shacking up with some guy for all we know."

"I don't think so. The place felt like nobody'd been there for a while."

I nodded in agreement. "But who turned the light on?"

Charlie didn't answer. I chewed on my lip for a minute, then said, "Oh, for Pete's sake. She was on vacation. She's using a timer switch so the lights will come on at night. If you don't, it's like putting out a welcome mat for the burglars."

"Let's go then," Charlie said. *"Just walk right to the door like you belong here. Don't act like you're trying not to be seen."*

"I wasn't born yesterday, Charlie." I got out of the car

and pulled the hood of my sweatshirt up to hide my hair. No one would think it was strange since it was a chilly spring night. As I walked up the stairs, I was really hoping the key I'd stolen wasn't Amanda's spare house key. Charlie wouldn't expect me to be able to pick a lock, would he? But the key fit perfectly. My knees felt a little rubbery.

I stepped inside and closed the door so quickly I closed it on Charlie. Not that he noticed. One of the lamps beside the couch was on. The apartment had the stale, airless feel of an empty building. The lights had been on in the apartment next door and I could hear the faint sound of a television. *"It's a good thing the light's on, Charlie. I didn't think about bringing a flashlight."*

"A flashlight'll bring the cops faster than lights going on. Let's see if she has a desk."

"Women don't keep secrets in desks. Let's look in her underwear drawers."

Her underwear drawers were full of nightgowns, half-slips, bras I could have wrapped around myself twice, and size nine panties. Size nine panties meant Amanda was a size eighteen. I don't know why panty sizes are different from pants sizes. I checked all the other drawers, finding scarves and gloves and sweaters and pantyhose and socks and hair curlers and makeup and a whole lot of other junk. I looked under the bed, staying down on all fours with my nose almost on the carpet until my eyes adjusted enough for me to see there wasn't anything under there. I'd turned on the hall light and left the bedroom door open, thinking that light would be less noticeable from outside.

"The closet," I said to Charlie.

The closet had its own light, a bare bulb with a long chain dangling from it. I stepped in and pulled the door mostly closed behind me, then gave the chain a yank. It wasn't really a walk-in closet, just a little bigger than usual with the clothes rod set back so there was space to stand in front of it. The rod was jam-packed with clothes, but I didn't see any reason to search through them. I started taking boxes off the closet shelf one at a time.

They were full of photographs, lots of them pictures of Jonathan when he was a child, and old bills, tax returns, Jonathan's high school report cards, letters, poems clipped from magazines, old address books, legal documents like Amanda and Charlie's and Amanda and George Reynolds's marriage certificates and divorce papers and Jonathan's birth certificate. *"The closet shelf's too obvious, Lizbet. As soon as she heard about Betty Yakamoto, she'd have come back home to hide them better."*

Charlie had a point, so I walked around the bedroom looking for a hiding place. Charlie kept telling me to look in the other rooms. *"Women hide things in their bedrooms, Charlie, trust me."*

I pressed my face against the wall next to the mirror connected to Amanda's dresser. *"Ah ha!"* I tugged the dresser out from the wall enough to reach my hand behind the mirror. A big flat manila envelope was taped to the back of the mirror.

There were three bright blue file folders in the envelope. I took them into the closet so I'd have enough light to read by. When I read the labels, my hands started shaking. BILBO, CHARLES; TOWNE, SAMUEL; KOSVAK, IVAN.

"Kosvak. That was the terrorist. Did you recommend your dentist to him, too?" I sounded really snotty, I know, but I was getting scared. Russians were heavy-duty bad guys in the 'sixties.

"No, I didn't. Take a look at his records." Charlie had been looking through ghost versions of the files.

I opened Charlie's file first. *"These aren't anything like the ones Sterling has. Look, there's your bridge."*

I opened Kosvak's file next. He'd only been to McMillan once, in May, 1969. He'd had a check-up, including x-rays. He had good teeth with only three fillings. *"This looks like the one Sterling showed me."*

"Check out Towne's."

Samuel Towne's teeth were noticeably crooked, especially his two top front teeth, which leaned toward one another. His eye teeth protruded and seemed longer than normal, almost like fangs. He was also missing two or three back teeth on each side.

"Your x-rays and Kosvak's were switched, so if your body had been discovered, the x-rays would seem to prove it wasn't really you. Amanda must have figured out they were switched after she went to work for Dr. McMillan. Why didn't she tell anyone? Why'd she keep all the files but never do anything about it?"

Charlie just shrugged. I looked at his x-ray again. Something about it bothered me. I couldn't figure it out for a moment, then I realized it was the handwriting. There was a space at the top where Charlie's name and the date were printed. Since it was done on the x-ray, the background was black and the letters were white. Charlie's name was printed very neatly in letters that were separate, but shaped more like cursive letters than printed letters. If you added strokes between them, they wouldn't look like printing.

I frowned and said, *"This is Amanda's handwriting, Charlie. It was on a lot of those papers in the box. But she didn't work there until after you died."*

Charlie smiled, not his little boy smile, not his regular smile, not his cop smile. It was a little, apologetic smile, like he was hoping I wouldn't get mad at him.

I forgot not to talk out loud. "You *lied* to me." I sounded like a little girl who just found out there isn't any Santa

Claus. "*Why?* What difference would it make if I knew she was working there?" I left the closet, suddenly not wanting to be that close to Charlie. I sat on the edge of Amanda's bed. Charlie stood in front of the closed closet door. I hadn't turned the light out and a thin line of white showed around the edges of the door.

"I suppose it wouldn't have made much difference, except that you would have figured it out sooner."

"What do you mean? I thought that's what you wanted."

"You had to trust me, to be willing to help me. I couldn't stay if you didn't want me to. It's a rule."

"But ... I would have still helped you. I don't understand, Charlie. What difference does it make when Amanda worked for McMillan? She was mixed up in it somehow, I understand that now. She switched the x-rays and kept quiet about it all these years."

Charlie didn't say anything. He just stood there looking at me with that same apologetic smile. Even in the dim light his eyes were bright blue and I had the oddest sensation that he was pinning me down with his eyes, that if I didn't move soon I wouldn't be able to move at all, that if I didn't look away, I'd be trapped forever. I raised my hand, shielding my eyes as if from a bright light. "Oh, Charlie. What else did you lie about?"

And still he didn't say anything. I forced myself to look away from his eyes, clenching my hands in my lap, watching my knuckles turn white.

"It's all a lie, isn't it? Everything you told me. All lies."

I heard a sigh and looked up. Charlie's eyes seemed to have dimmed, to have lost their power. He touched the peace symbol on his chest and said, *"Not all of it."* Then he laughed and added, *"Just the important parts."*

I felt a tear dribble down my cheek. I guess even ghosts

aren't always what they seem. "That cop didn't fall asleep. It *was* you who drove out of the warehouse at two o'clock. You did it, didn't you? You stole the money and blew up the building and killed those cops."

He didn't deny it. I felt something awful happen inside me, my heart breaking, or maybe just the death of the very last tiny bit of unquestioning trust I had left over from my childhood. When I spoke, my voice sounded strange, hollow and empty. "You might as well tell me the whole story."

"The cops dying wasn't part of my plan. It was Towne and Kosvak I was after. They were anarchists, both of them, plotting destruction and death, not caring who they hurt as long as they could pursue their goals. I didn't have any qualms about killing them. I thought—I convinced myself that killing them, that ridding the world of two evil men would justify my actions. But ... it was the money I was after."

"Money. Oh, Charlie."

"It all started with the x-rays. That's funny, isn't it? Because it's probably going to end with them, too." And then he told me the whole story, the true story.

Chapter Twenty-one

It started with the x-rays. In 1969 Amanda had been work-ing for James McMillan for three years. In January she asked Charlie about a man named Samuel Towne, who had had an appointment that day. On the form he filled out for the den-tist, he'd given Charlie's name as the person who referred him. Towne didn't know Charlie's real name, of course, but Amanda recognized the phony name he was using for the undercover assignment.

"Amanda knew he had to be connected with the case I was work-ing on and she was curious. She was also fascinated by him. Towne wasn't good-looking, but there was something about him, a sort of charisma. A requirement for an ambitious radical activist, I suppose. You have to be able to draw people to you and make them follow you blindly. Whatever the quality is, Towne had it. Amanda kept telling me he had strange eyes. Crazy eyes, that's how she described them."

Like Charles Manson, I thought. Crazy eyes. Killer eyes.

Charlie rarely discussed the details of his undercover work with Amanda but he found himself telling her about Towne and Kosvak and the kidnapping plot. That's when the idea first came to him. It was just a crazy thought, more of a fantasy than anything else, a wild idea, almost a joke. Charlie said he could steal the money and kill Towne, making sure body was in such shape he could only be identified by dental x-rays. Amanda could make a switch—Charlie's x-rays for Towne's x-rays—and the cops would identify the body as Charlie. Officially dead, Charlie would hide somewhere, wait a few weeks for Amanda and their little son to join him, and they'd go someplace far away—another country, an island in the South Pacific maybe, a place where they could establish new identities and live like royalty on the money.

"I wasn't serious," Charlie said. *"It was just one of those crazy ideas that pop into your head. But Amanda got all excited. She kept telling me it would work. I could tell she actually wanted to do it. I told her it wouldn't work, because of Towne's teeth being so crooked. If anyone who knew me saw his body, or saw the x-rays, they'd know it couldn't be me. My teeth are straight. Except for the bridge, they're in good shape. It was too risky to try to pass his x-rays off as mine."*

Charlie thought that was the end of it. Every once in a while Amanda would mention it, saying how wonderful it would be to have all that money and start a whole new life. Early in May she came home from work and told Charlie that Ivan Kosvak had an appointment that day and she'd taken x-rays. Samuel Towne had referred him to Dr. McMillan.

"Looking back now," Charlie said, *"I know that getting Kosvak to go to McMillan was all part of Towne's plan. Kosvak was a hypochondriac. He was always swallowing aspirin and taking his own temperature and pulse and worrying about catching something. Towne probably mentioned something about his teeth. Maybe he told him it looked like he was developing gum disease. Kosvak would have panicked. Towne gave him McMillan's name. It's funny, you never think of terrorists doing something as mundane as going to the dentist."*

Amanda told Charlie that Kosvak showing up in McMillan's dental chair was a sign, a sign with a capital S. She said Charlie could kill both Towne and Kosvak. Charlie's x-rays could be switched with Kosvak's. Since they both had nice straight teeth, no one would question the x-rays. Charlie would be officially dead, they'd have the money, they'd be rich and free to start over someplace else. Charlie thought it over and the more he thought it over, the more he thought it would work.

"*All that money,*" Charlie said. "*Who could resist it?*"

"Everyone *wants* money, Charlie. Most people won't kill for it."

"*But all I had to do was kill two men who didn't deserve to live anyway. They were terrorists, Lizbet, fanatics who didn't care how many innocent bystanders they destroyed. And I was tired of being a cop, tired of dealing with scum and putting in fifty or sixty hours a week for peanuts. It seemed perfect. The world would be better off with Towne and Kosvak dead and we'd have the money.*

"*So I came up with a plan. I would have preferred to do it weeks earlier, but Kosvak wouldn't bring the money to the warehouse until just before the kidnapping. I ended up doing it the same night the bust was scheduled. It's funny, if it had worked out the way I planned it, everything might have been screwed up because of Aguilar getting a good look at me when I left. I didn't think anyone would be able to tell who was driving the Volkswagen. Of course, the way it turned out, it was just more evidence that I took the money and ran.*

"*Kosvak was at the warehouse with me that night, guarding the money. We were the only ones there after midnight, but I told the SWAT team that some other guards would be there, too, just to confuse things. Towne was supposed to arrive at three in the morning. Kosvak and Towne were the only ones who knew the combination to the safe. I got it out of Kosvak. It took me half an hour. You don't want to hear the details.*"

I was sure I didn't. I tried hard not to even think about what he meant, but I felt sick all the same.

"*Anyway, Kosvak was in bad shape. I should have killed him then, I guess, but I just tied him up. I didn't want there to be any question about the time of death. I wanted him to die in the explo-*

sion, not before it. After I got the money from the safe, I set up the bomb. I'd planned to connect it to the automatic door opener, but the wiring system was confusing and I wasn't sure I could do it, so I rigged a trip-wire instead. Too bad: the cops wouldn't have died if I'd been able to use the door opener to detonate the bomb.

"Towne was supposed to come to the warehouse at three, like I said. When no one opened the door for him, he'd assume we'd fallen asleep. It had happened before, so he wouldn't be suspicious. He'd open the door himself and set off the bomb when he walked in and he and Kosvak would die. Since Amanda was supposed to put Kosvak's x-rays in my file, the cops would think it was me and Towne who died. They'd be looking for Kosvak. It seemed like a foolproof plan. I'd have the money and no one would be looking for me. Amanda was going to wait a month then meet me in Miami. We were going to leave the country from there."

"Your foolproof plan killed two cops, Charlie."

He sighed. *"It was my bust, Lizbet, I'd set it all up. We'd gone over the details a hundred times. I was supposed to leave at two, then come back at two-thirty after calling in a report. I told them over and over that if I didn't leave at two or I didn't make the call or I didn't come back at two-thirty, if anything didn't go down just the way it was supposed to, they were to pull out and we'd come up with another plan.*

"The shape Kosvak was in, I was sure he'd be unconscious for hours. But I guess he came to and somehow managed to reach the switch for the door. His timing couldn't have been worse. At two-thirty he opened the door and the SWAT team was still there and like fools they went on in. Towne was supposed to trip the bomb when he arrived at three. Instead, the cops tripped it half an hour before he was due to arrive."

"So it was Kosvak's body in the building. But he was identified as Towne, not as you."

Charlie smiled. A cop smile. Or maybe a killer smile. *"Of course. Because my beloved wife Amanda double-crossed me."*

The way Charlie figured it, Amanda had fallen for Towne. He had several dental appointments after the first one in January, so the opportunity existed. Towne and Amanda got together, probably became lovers, and Amanda told him about Charlie's wild idea to kill him and take the money. Amanda and Samuel Towne made a plan of their own.

Amanda made a three-way switch: Kosvak's x-rays went into Charlie's file. Charlie's x-rays went into Towne's file. Towne's x-rays went into Kosvak's file. So Kosvak's body was identified as Samuel Towne and if Charlie's body happened to be found, the teeth would be compared to Kosvak's x-rays and no one would ever know it was really Charlie.

"It was better, of course, if my body was never found. I don't know what Van Horne's connection was with Towne. They must have known each other at college. Maybe Towne had something on him and blackmailed him into helping dispose of my body. Your backyard was perfect."

"Is that where you were killed? In my backyard?"

"No. When I left the warehouse at two o'clock, I drove to an abandoned garage a few miles away. I had stored some paint there and license plates so I could disguise the car enough to drive it out of the state before I got rid of it. I had things there to change my appearance, too, hair dye and a fake beard and glasses. I pulled into the garage and closed the door, then all of a sudden I heard someone behind me. It was Towne and he had a gun. I understood everything then. I knew Amanda had crossed me because she was the only person who knew where the garage was. Towne had rigged up a phone and he made me call her. He told me exactly what to say."

"And what was that?"

"I said, 'It didn't work, Amanda. Towne's dead and I've got the money.' That was all. Towne yanked the phone cord loose and put the gun against the back of my head and pulled the trigger."

I leaned over for a moment, my face in my hands. When

I felt better, I raised up and looked at Charlie. "So Amanda thought you killed Towne and got rid of his body and ran off with the money. And she couldn't go to the cops without telling them she was involved in the whole thing."

"Right."

"She kept duplicate files all these years, so if you ever turned up, she could prove who you were and she could prove it wasn't Towne but Kosvak who died in the explosion."

"Yeah, I suppose that's why she kept them."

"Why did everyone believe Kosvak's body was really Samuel Towne? Didn't anyone notice that Towne's teeth straightened out when he died? That's why you couldn't pass Towne's x-rays off as yours, so why didn't someone figure out that the body in the warehouse couldn't be him?"

"The medical examiner and anyone else who was likely to look at the x-rays knew me, but they didn't know Towne. Even if they saw a picture of him, they wouldn't notice his teeth. He was very self-conscious about them. He seldom smiled and barely moved his lips when he talked. Only someone who'd been around him a lot would know about his teeth, and no one who knew him would ever have any reason to look at the x-rays. McMillan's office gave the cops some dental records with Samuel Towne's name on them and the x-rays matched the teeth of body in the warehouse. Why would they question it? No one would have any reason to suspect a dentist of switching records."

"All these years, Amanda thought it was you who cheated her out of the money, but it was really Towne. Do you suppose he's still alive?"

"I don't know. It seems strange that he's never turned up, but I suppose it's possible. He was younger than me. He'd be in his early fifties now and a million dollars would buy a lot of dental work and plastic surgery."

I stood up, feeling stiff. My hands were icy. It was two

o'clock in the morning. Charlie was still standing in front of the closet, the white light around the edges of the door framing him. I brushed a tear off each cheek. "Duke used to talk about the 'sixties all the time. He made it sound like it was all peace and love, hippies with love beads and flowers in their hair holding hands and singing songs, trying to make the world a better place. What a lie. You were a real nice bunch of people, weren't you? Thieves and killers, just out to get whatever you could, not caring how you got it. You plotted to kill Towne, and Towne and Amanda double-crossed you, then Towne double-crossed Amanda. Peace and love. What a joke."

"I was no flower child, Lizbet. I was a cop—"

"You were a killer."

"—and I busted hippies every chance I got. I know you're disappointed in me. I had to lie. If I'd told you the truth, you'd never have agreed to help me. I couldn't stay here unless you were willing to let me."

I stared at him. Charlie Bilbo with his bright blue eyes and pale blond hair and hippie threads, Horst Martinez's silver and turquoise pendant against his chest. A symbol of peace, worn by a man who dealt in betrayal. "You're a killer, Charlie. A killer and a torturer and a thief and a cheat. You're also a ghost. What was it you told me? I can just tell you to go away?"

Something close to panic crossed Charlie's face, and he reached a hand out toward me. *"Don't, Lizbet. You need me. You can't explain how you knew the bones were mine unless I stay here. Sterling—"*

"Sterling's a cop, not a ghost." I faced him squarely and looked into his eyes. "Maybe I can't get away from a cop, but I can get away from you. I don't want you here, Charlie Bilbo. You aren't welcome in my universe. Go away."

"NO! LIZ—"

And he was gone.

Chapter Twenty-two

I cried after Charlie went away. It wasn't one of my famous crying jags, which Lady always said were pure self-indul-
gence anyway. I just sat on the bed in Amanda Reynolds's
dark bedroom, staring at the closet door with its outline of
white light while tears ran down my cheeks, and into my nose.
Crying would be a lot nicer if your nose didn't have anything
to do with it.

I wasn't thinking about Charlie at first, or Amanda or
Samuel Towne or Captain Sterling or even what I was going to
do now. I thought about me, about all the wrong choices I
made and the wrong men I'd known. I've always been a loser-
magnet, attracting bad men and worthless men and lying men.
I always trust them, even when the evidence of their deceit is
staring me right in the face.

I thought about the last time I saw Duke and Lady. We had
a fight, a terrible, hurtful fight. They only wanted to make me
see the latest loser for what he really was, but I wouldn't listen
and said lots of things I didn't really mean, knowing that later
on I could tell them I was sorry and they'd forgive me because
they always did. But weeks went by, months actually, and I
never got around to it and then they were dead and it was too
late and I'm going to spend the rest of my life knowing that
the last words I said to them were *Get out of my life.*

I should have said that to all the losers but I said it Duke and Lady instead and now I'd said the same thing to Charlie. Well, not exactly the same words, but you know what I mean. And now Charlie was gone. Out of my life.

I checked my watch. It was almost three, the dead of the night. I shivered suddenly, thinking about leaving Amanda's apartment and walking down a dark stairway and across a dark, deserted parking lot. If Charlie'd been with me, I wouldn't have been scared, which was really funny since I could have been attacked by a deranged homicidal maniac and Charlie couldn't do anything but stand there and watch.

I sighed and plucked one more Kleenex out of the box on Amanda's nightstand to give my nose a final blow. I gathered up all the used tissues, then turned out the closet light, shoved the dresser back against the wall, and left the bedroom, carrying the manila envelope containing the three file folders. I decided I wouldn't leave until dawn. Where was I going to go anyway? If I went home, I'd probably have a big fight with Jonathan. I didn't think I could deal with him right now, especially now that I knew what his mother had done. While Charlie was telling his story, telling the truth, it hadn't really hit me too hard. But afterward, it did. Amanda had conspired with her lover to kill her husband, to murder her son's father. I shivered every time I thought of it. And that woman was sleeping in one of my beds! I'd have to burn the sheets.

The hall light was still on, but the timer had turned the lamp in the living room off. There was plenty of light, though. The draperies weren't thick and the moonlight filtered through them. I stopped briefly in the bathroom to throw the tissues away, not even caring what Amanda thought when she found ten or fifteen used tissues in her formerly empty wastebasket. I walked quietly through the empty apartment, the kitchen first, where I got a drink of water, then the living room. A tiny blinking light caught my eye: Amanda's answering machine, signaling a message. Two messages, I saw when I got closer. The phone hadn't rung so the calls had come before we arrived. With the lamp on, neither of us had noticed the little light.

I found the volume control first and turned it almost all the way down, then touched the message button. The first call was from Captain Sterling, asking her to call him. So, he'd tracked down the mysterious Mandy Reynolds. I wondered if he'd found out yet that she was Jonathan Dillon's mother and Charlie Bilbo's wife. He sounded very polite and formal, so I thought he probably hadn't.

The second message scared the hell out of me: *It's me, Mandy. You were Clitty-Clitty and I was Dong-Dong, remember? A real blast from the past, right? If you haven't already fainted, listen hard—honesty isn't the best policy, silence is. Don't make me mad.*

My knees were shaking so hard I had to sit down. Samuel Towne! It had to be Samuel Towne, the man Amanda believed had been murdered by her husband. Who else would be such a blast from the past that Amanda would faint from shock? Samuel Towne, alive and somewhere nearby, because how else could he know what was going on? How else could he know that after twenty-seven years, Amanda was suddenly a threat to him?

I pressed my knuckles against my mouth, panic, like a cold finger on my spine, sending shudders through my body. Towne could be outside right now, in the parking lot, waiting for Amanda to come home. There was a phone attached to the answering machine of course, but I went back to the kitchen where I'd seen one on the wall. It was lighter in there, the curtains thinner, letting in more moonlight. There was also a back door in the kitchen, with a window in it. I'd peeked out earlier and seen the steep stairway leading to the ground below. I liked the idea of being near the back door, just in case someone came knocking on the front door.

I called my house. Jonathan answered on the first ring.

I whispered, "It's me, Jonathan. Listen—"

"Goddammit, Lizbet, where are you?" He sounded wide awake and mad as hell.

"Jonathan, don't let Amanda out of your sight. She's in danger, terrible danger."

"Where are you?"

"I can't tell you, just be sure—"

"You tell me where you are. You can't just—"

I hung up the phone very quietly and backed away, my heart pounding, my stomach doing flip-flops. I'd heard a creak, the sound of wood reacting to weight. I heard another. And then another. Oh, god, someone was coming up the back steps.

I tiptoed to the living room and popped the miniature tape out of the answering machine and picked up the manila envelope. I looked out the peep hole on the front door. All I saw was the empty walkway. A voice in my mind screamed *There could be more than one of them!* but I didn't pay any attention to it, because I'd heard a new sound, the sound of a doorknob being jiggled. The person at the back door was real. What was out the front door was unknown. I opted for the unknown and eased the door open.

I closed it behind me as quietly as I could and started down the stairs. I wanted to run but I forced myself to go slowly, quietly. When I got to the bottom, I pulled my keys from my pocket and walked to the car, moving faster now because whoever was at Amanda's back door couldn't even know for sure I'd been in her apartment. I was just a woman dressed in black, a hood hiding her hair, hurrying across a dark parking lot in the middle of the night. Lights were on in a few of the apartments, insomniacs or early-risers or lights on timers—I didn't know which, but the lights made me feel safer. Just as I reached the Volvo, a car passed by on the street, twangy country music trailing behind it.

I started the engine immediately, turning the headlights on and opening the window a few inches, then I turned the radio on and jacked the volume way up. A woman running away, sneaking away, wouldn't play her radio too loud. I wasn't running away, I wasn't afraid, I was just some woman driving away, not caring if she woke up everyone with her radio blaring rock music in the middle of the night. I pulled out of the parking place, glancing at Amanda's front window. I thought the curtain moved a bit but it might have been my imagination.

I was a couple blocks away when I started laughing hysterically. Clitty-Clitty and Dong-Dong! I could just hear the two of them together: Here, Clitty-Clitty! Heeere, Clitty-Clitty! Oh, Dong-Dong, ooohhh, Dong-Dong, oooooooohhhh, Doooooong-Dong!

I kept laughing, choking and gasping and snorting, helpless to stop, laughing until I was screaming with laughter, tears rolling down my cheeks, my sides aching. I laughed right up until the siren scared the shit out of me and blue light flashed through the interior of the car. I pulled over and turned the radio off.

The San Jose cop told me I'd been driving erratically, weaving across the lane. He leaned down toward me, checking for booze on my breath. I deliberately heaved a big sigh right in his face and told him I had allergies and I'd had a sneezing fit. He examined my license and registration and insurance card, then told me to pull over to the side of the road if I started sneezing again. A tiny tape with a murderer's threat on it was in my pocket and file folders with the dental records of two murdered men and a killer were on the seat beside me. I smiled at the nice policeman and promised him I would.

Chapter Twenty-three

The parking lot of Tony's Truck Stop was nearly deserted. Two big rigs were parked in the rear of the lot, engines running. There were only two cars and I recognized them both. The battered blue pickup belonged to Raoul, the night-shift cook, and the blue Yugo with the smashed fender was Melissa's.

I never thought Melissa's name fit her. She needed a harder name—Gertrude or Roberta maybe—to go with her bony body and the deep lines around her mouth. Melissa tells everyone the same sad story. She got married young to a guy named Patrick O'Neal, a red-headed Irishman. They had two children, then Patrick died in a car accident and she had to fend for herself and raise the children alone. Her daughter is fifteen and her son is sixteen. Melissa turned thirty just before I quit working at Tony's, which means she had to have gotten married when she was about thirteen. Her daughter has dark skin and black hair and deep brown eyes, definitely Hispanic. Her son is half black. No one I know ever had the guts to question Melissa's sad story. There's something about her eyes that makes you think of sharp things, like butcher knives and meat cleavers and ice picks.

She gave me a tired smile, brushing a wisp of dry sandy hair away from her forehead with the back of her hand. "How's it going?" she said, not seeming at all surprised to see me at four in the morning after not seeing me for weeks and weeks.

"Fine," I said and ordered coffee and toast.

When she brought it, she slid into the booth across from me and brought me up to date on the goings-on at Tony's. The same old stuff. Lisa was pregnant and Marty was getting divorced and Raoul had been in jail again and Mickey had his driver's license revoked and Andy's wife dumped the kids on him and ran off with a trucker named Joe-Pete. After a while Melissa left to clear tables and wait on the few customers straggling in. I was so tired my mind didn't seem to be working. My thoughts just went in circles. I finally decided to check into a motel and get some sleep, but I made the mistake of leaning my head against the wall for just a moment and that was all it took.

I woke up when Melissa touched my shoulder. "Breakfast crowd's starting to come in, honey." I nodded and slid out of the booth. I splashed water on my face in the bathroom and got a cup of coffee to go. I felt like something no self-respecting cat would bother to drag in.

Tony's is on the south side of San Jose. I drove north to the airport and left the Volvo in the long-term parking lot. Then I found out car rental places won't take cash, only credit cards. Jeez! I took a cab to a body shop that runs a rent-a-clunker business as a sideline. I used to date a guy who worked there and I knew they liked cash a lot more than plastic. They gave me a banged-up old blue Ford with a broken side-view mirror on the passenger side and stuffing coming out of the seat. I headed toward downtown and got a room at a cheap motel, asking for a wake-up call at nine o'clock. Between renting the car and paying for the room, the money I'd stuck in my pocket was nearly gone.

When the phone rang, I really had to force myself to get up, but after a shower I felt pretty good for only having three and a half hours' sleep, not counting the nap at the truck stop. I found a branch office of my bank and after I convinced them I was really me even though I didn't have a checkbook or bankbook or credit card with me, just a driver's license, they very kindly let me have some of my own money. I went on a shopping spree at K-Mart.

Less than an hour after I got back to the motel, I was ready to leave. I studied my reflection in the full-length mirror on the bathroom door. My hair was a dull medium brown. According to the box, the shampoo-in color would wash right out again. I had used styling gel on the front section, making it stand stiffly upward, like the law of gravity had been repealed. I had let the rest of my hair dry uncombed, so it was a tangle of loose curls. I had applied makeup heavily, darkening my eyebrows, painting my eyelids vivid blue, and giving my cheeks a clownish blush. I put on so much mascara it was a wonder I could hold my eyelids open. I was wearing purple pants with a wide white belt, a matching blouse in a bright purple and pink floral print, and white sandals. I looked really tacky.

I put my driver's license and money and Amanda's key in a white fake-leather shoulder bag along with a powder compact, a comb, a pack of gum, a small notebook, a pen, and a pair of sunglasses. I added some Kleenex from a dispenser in the bathroom. Everything else—the clothes I'd been wearing, makeup, another new pants and top outfit in gaudy green and blue, the three file folders, and the miniature tape sealed inside a motel envelope—went into a big straw tote-bag with some flashy sequined flowers on front. One last glance in the mirror convinced me that I looked like someone else. I drove off in the rented Ford, heading toward Oak Valley, wondering what on earth I was doing.

Actually, I knew exactly what I was doing—I was acting like I was running from the cops. On the lam. Well, I was in a way, and it didn't seem fair at all. I hadn't done anything wrong, unless you count housebreaking and theft, and for Pete's sake I only did it because Charlie told me to. I especially wanted to avoid two particular cops—Jonathan and Captain Sterling. It had occurred to me at the truck stop that either one of them could get the Volvo's license plate number and ask their cop buddies to keep an eye out for it. They could probably even have an APB broadcast, asking every cop in the state to be on the lookout for me.

I was also nervous about Van Horne. If he helped bury Charlie's body, he had a good reason to want to keep me quiet. Sterling must have told him all about me knowing things I shouldn't know about Charlie Bilbo. Thinking about Charlie made me feel weepy. I missed him. I was also worried because now I knew lots of things with no earthly explanation. Charlie was supposed to tie up all the loose ends before he left, and now there were loose ends hanging out all over the place. I wondered if he'd get in trouble. I couldn't imagine what kind of trouble, unless it had something to do with shoveling fiery coals.

I was almost to Oak Valley when I remembered something Jonathan said—we had to figure out who the weak link was. I suspected the weakest link was Amanda. If I played the answering machine tape for her, she'd probably spill her guts. But Jonathan was with her and he'd butt right in and there wouldn't be any way I could keep him from listening to the tape. He'd have to know eventually about his mother and Samuel Towne, but nobody should have to hear a man referring to his mother as Clitty-Clitty. It could be really traumatic. Deep down inside I don't even believe Duke and Lady actually did it. Except once to have me and I kind of lean toward immaculate conception anyway.

Maybe Van Horne was a weak link. He'd been a cop for years and years and was about to become the Chief of Police. If he helped Towne get rid of Charlie's body, Towne had a real strong hold over him now. If he thought I could expose him anyway, he might rat on Towne. Van Horne was a cop though, and cops scare me. I couldn't figure out how to approach him anyway. I was afraid to show anyone the x-rays, even Captain Sterling, until I knew for sure who the good guys were. Van Horne could just take them away from me and then there wouldn't be any kind of proof at all.

I finally decided Horst Martinez would have to be my weak link. I couldn't figure out exactly how he was involved in the whole thing, but he definitely knew what really happened to Charlie.

I took the exit for downtown Oak Valley and found a parking spot by the campus, hoping he'd be there again. He was. There were five or six other people in the room on the second floor. They all looked like college kids except for an older woman who was ordering everyone around. When she spotted me, she made a shooing gesture at me. "The display opens tomorrow at one," she said.

"I'm a friend of Horst's," I said. She gave me a really haughty look. I knew exactly what she was thinking: *Cheap little tramp.*

Martinez had heard his name and hurried right over, practically drooling, which sure didn't say much about his taste in women. I was wearing the sunglasses, which had huge round black lenses. I snapped the big wad of gum in my mouth and said, "Hi, Horst, how's it going?," making my voice loud and kind of crude-sounding, not at all like my normal sweet voice.

Martinez was wearing blue denim overalls today, with a dark blue T-shirt. I could see him trying to place me, without any luck. He put his arm around my waist, giving me a quick hug, saying, "Fine, fine, just finishing up in here ... uh ..." He was groping for a name, but I didn't help him out. "I could use a break. Why don't I buy you something to drink at the Student Union?"

I took his arm and smiled at him. "Sure, Horst, honey. We got a lot to talk about, don't we?"

He looked a little uneasy, licking his lips and giving the older woman an anxious glance. I didn't give him a chance to change his mind. I gave his arm a yank and headed toward the door, walking fast, practically running down the stairs with him panting beside me.

The Student Union was across a wide grassy area. We walked past the bookstore and went into the cafeteria. Martinez kept looking at me like a little bell was tinkling somewhere in the back of his mind. I told him I just wanted a Coke and hurried off to find a table, leaving him in line.

The place was crowded. There were noisy groups of students gathered at most of the tables, all of them talking at once. Straw wrappers floated in the air, which struck me as a lot more like high school than college. I was glad the place was crowded. Martinez could hardly choke me to death with so many people watching.

I found a table for two and cleared away the trays and plates and wadded napkins someone had left—it doesn't matter what I do, I always end up bussing tables—then I sat down and checked on Martinez's progress in the line. He must have been well known on the campus. Several students went up to talk to him while he was working his way down to the cash register end of the counter. A guy with his head shaved except for a real long section sprouting from the top of his head carried the tray to the table, yapping to Martinez the whole time. I was afraid he was going to join us but Martinez told him he'd catch him later.

I wrapped my gum in a napkin and took a drink of the Coke he placed in front of me. "I have to apologize," he said. "I'm afraid your name escapes me."

I thought about asking how he could possibly forget me after that incredible night we spent together and then telling him I flunked my HIV test, but that seemed a little juvenile, so instead I leaned toward him and spoke in a whisper: "Samuel Towne killed Charlie Bilbo in nineteen sixty-nine. Charlie's body was buried behind a house up in the Foothills. The place was recommended by Theodore Van Horne, who was working for the landscaping company that was doing the yard work. The body in the warehouse was really Ivan Kosvak, a terrorist. Samuel Towne is still alive. You got back the peace symbol you gave to Charlie. You were photographed wearing it in nineteen eighty-eight. You know Charlie Bilbo was murdered."

I leaned back to see what his reaction would be.

It was a little different than I expected. He'd listened without much expression at all, his face just getting a little pale and sweaty. He had automatically leaned forward when I started whispering so we'd been almost nose to nose. When I finished, he leaned back, his mouth opening. Then he gasped loudly, clutched his chest, and fell out of the chair. I stood up, pushing my chair back so fast that it tipped over, hitting the tile floor with a loud metallic clang. Someone shouted "Hey!" and all of a sudden there were people shoving against me, crowding around Horst Martinez, who was sprawled on his back on the floor making horrible squeaky gasping sounds, his hands clutching at his chest.

I started backing away, bumping into people and sidestepping around them. People were shouting and a skinny girl with bright red hair was screaming non-stop, her mouth wide open, showing teeth full of silver fillings. I turned around and fought my way out of the building, pushing through crowds of people who were rushing in to see what all the commotion was about. I headed back toward my car, my heart pounding, the straw tote bag banging against my knees, my purse dragging on the ground because the strap had slipped off my shoulder and was hooked on my wrist. I jerked it up and clutched the straw tote against my chest and ran.

Oh, god, I killed Horst Martinez!

Chapter Twenty-four

My hands and knees were shaking so bad I could hardly drive. I only went a few blocks, stopping at a gas station where I got the key to the women's room. I changed into the blue and green outfit and yanked a comb through the gelled section of my hair. After I got the top flattened, I combed all the rest. Instead of tangled curls, I had loose brown waves. I left the sunglasses off. I'd parked as close to the door as I could, hoping no one at the station would see me leave in my new disguise. I didn't see anyone looking at me.

I drove a few more blocks and stopped at a convenience store with a phone attached to the outside wall. I called my house. Jonathan answered right away.

"Oh, god, Jonathan—"

"*Lizbet!* Goddammit, where are you? I almost shot your cleaning people when they came in at six-thirty in the morning without even knocking."

"Oh, is it Thursday? Well, they have keys. I'm not usually awake that early so they just come on in. I'm sorry, I should have told you. Jonathan, something awful—"

"Where are you?"

"I killed someone. At least, I think I killed him. Maybe they can do CPR or something, but he looked awful."

I heard Jonathan breathing for a moment. "You *what?*"

"Um ... I think I killed someone. What am I going to do?"

"Killed someone? Who? How'd you kill him?"

With words. I killed him with words. Did words count as a deadly weapon? Could I help it if his heart blew up? Was that my fault? Maybe nobody could blame me.

Jonathan's voice was very gentle, like he was talking to a skittish animal, or maybe a moron: "Just tell me what happened, Lizbet. I'll help you."

I hung up. The receiver smelled like sour breath anyway and was making me sick to my stomach. I got back in the car, but I didn't start the engine. An ambulance coming from the direction of the college sped past, siren wailing, heading toward St. Anthony's. Would they use the siren if he was dead? I wasn't sure. Maybe a doctor has to officially declare people dead before they stop trying to save them.

I forced myself to stop worrying about Martinez so I could figure out what to do. The cops thought Samuel Towne was dead and Charlie was alive. I knew Towne killed Charlie, but I couldn't prove it and I couldn't even tell anyone because there wasn't any way for me to know it. I had the x-rays, of course, but who was I supposed to give them to? The cops already had x-rays they believed were the real ones. How could I prove the ones I had weren't phony?

I chewed on my thumbnail. How did I get in this mess anyway? All I wanted was a swimming pool. Now I'd lied to just about everybody I talked to since Monday and I stole a key and broke into an apartment and swiped a tape and some dental records and made a famous artist have a heart attack and colored my hair ugly brown and almost got my cleaning team shot by a cop. If the color didn't wash out,

Monsieur Jacques would have a fit. He always raved about the color of my hair. I spit out a tiny bit of nail polish. Now the manicurist was going to be mad at me, too. This was all Charlie's fault. I sighed and started the car and drove to the library. Duke always used to say a little knowledge might be a dangerous thing but it's better than being stupid.

I started with January of 1969, popping the cassette into the microfiche machine and watching newspaper headlines flash by like ghosts of old tragedies. There are hardly ever any happy stories in the newspaper. Except on New Year's Day when they print a picture of the first baby born after midnight. The first baby born on January 1, 1969 was the son of Rita Munoz, age fifteen, whose address was in the worst part of town. I bet that really pissed off a few people back then, the illegitimate child of a teenage welfare-mother making the front page of the *Oak Valley Journal.*

On January tenth, I found a whole page of pictures of cops who had just graduated from the Police Academy. I was on January twelfth before the significance of it hit me. I backtracked to the tenth. Theodore Van Horne was in the last row. He had light hair and eyes and a typical cop face—strong jaw, thick neck, eyes set close together. He looked familiar, which wasn't surprising. If he was about to become Chief of Police, he'd probably been on the news and in the paper hundreds of times. I never pay much attention to the news, except for the real juicy stuff like love-triangle murders and suicide pacts and priests being arrested for molesting children.

I left the machine on and got last Sunday's paper from the Recent Periodicals shelf, which a snooty librarian pointed out to me like I should have already known about it. I hurried back to the microfiche machine so no one would grab my place. Sure enough, there was a picture of both Van Horne and Chief of Police Winston Miller. Van Horne hadn't changed much. His hair was probably going gray, but the picture was black and white so I couldn't tell. He had some lines across his forehead and was a little jowly, but that was all. The story was boring. They'd attended some kind of charitable event. Miller's upcoming retirement was mentioned, as well as the fact that Van Horne would be replacing him. "Not if I can help it," I said. A man at a study carrel turned around and glared at me, clearing his throat loudly. Jeez, he'd made more noise than I had.

I looked at the picture of Winston Miller for a while. I'd seen him plenty of times. He was always on the news, gabbing about something or other. I'd always thought he was a strange-looking man. His features didn't seem to go together. His chin was too strong for his nose, which was so perfectly shaped it would have looked better on a woman, and his lips were too thin. He looked like he'd been put together from spare parts. He was always smiling, a big toothy smile, show-ing off perfect teeth. Probably capped. Nobody comes with teeth that good. He had deep-set brown eyes that always made me uncomfortable when I saw him on television, the kind of eyes people call piercing, like he could see right through you and knew what you were thinking. Hypnotic eyes.

Hypnotic eyes. Crazy eyes. *Killer eyes.* Like Charles Manson, oh my god, it's *him.*

I told myself it couldn't be true.

I told myself that a dozen times. Then I went to ask the librarian about the index for the *Journal* that she'd mentioned the first time I used the microfiche, when Charlie was with me. After she showed me how to use it, I got out my little notebook and copied the dates of the references to Winston Miller. There were so many in the last ten years, I didn't bother writing them down. The man was *always* in the paper. I vaguely remembered hearing something about him being considered as a candidate for senator or governor or something. I settled down in front of the machine again.

Winston Miller joined the Oak Valley Police Department in March, 1972, at the age of twenty-eight. He had previously been employed by the New York City Police Department for seven years.

"Well, phooey," I said. The guy in the carrel hissed *Shhh!* at me.

The age was right, but I didn't think he could lie about working in New York City. You can't just claim you've been a cop for seven years and get hired, can you? They'd check, wouldn't they? So I had to be wrong.

I read the rest of the articles anyway. In March, 1975, Miller made the front page. According to the article, he had almost single-handedly exposed a major dope ring, resulting in the arrest of two major dealers. In April of that year, he was promoted to sergeant. The article said it was a meritorious promotion, which I guess meant he hadn't been on the force long enough to be promoted just because of his experience. The promotion was sort of a reward for a job well done.

In April, 1977, Miller was promoted again, to detective sergeant, this time for almost single-handedly uncovering a major chop-shop operation.

In August, 1980, Miller made lieutenant. Guess what? Another major drug ring broken by the intrepid Winston Miller. Was this guy a white knight or what?

In July, 1984, Lieutenant Miller became Captain Miller. Much was made of the fact that he was the youngest captain ever in Oak Valley. I added it up and decided he was thirty-nine then.

He remained a captain, heading various departments and always getting awards for this and that, until 1988 when he was promoted to Deputy Chief of Police, replacing a man named Carl Connigan who had died in a car accident.

In 1990, Chief of Police Geraldo Escondido died in a hunting accident and—surprise, surprise—Winston Miller took his place. An interesting little sidebar to that story told how Theodore Van Horne was going to step into the Deputy Chief position. Van Horne had been a cop since 1969 and had almost as many meritorious service awards as Miller. Both of them seemed to have a real knack for uncovering drug rings and car theft rings and burglary rings and porno rings and so on.

Now Winston Miller was getting ready to retire and go into politics and Theodore Van Horne was going to take his place as Chief of Police. The newspaper stories gave me the impression that Van Horne had always ridden on Miller's coat-tails. In a lot of the stories about Miller, Van Horne was mentioned as assisting him or being on the scene or playing a crucial part in the preliminary investigation that led to the arrests.

Van Horne was moonlighting for Braverman's Landscaping when Charlie was buried in my backyard, six months after he graduated from the Police Academy. I hadn't come across anything else about him until after Winston Miller joined the force and then Van Horne cropped up constantly as Miller's sidekick. If Van Horne knew where a body was buried and knew Winston Miller was responsible for the body, Miller would want to keep him happy—and quiet.

But Winston Miller had worked for the New York City Police Department for seven years before he showed up in Oak Valley. I was shaking my head, thinking I had to be wrong, when I remembered the money. A million dollars. In 1969 it would have been worth even more than it is today.

Grandma Rose bought a house in 1965, a real nice house, and only paid twelve thousand for it. She's always telling me how you can't even get a decent car for that now. You can buy anything with a million dollars. Plastic surgery, phony identification, an entire background littered with fake, authentic-looking documentation. Why not a job history?

Almost three years passed between the time Samuel Towne supposedly died in a warehouse in Oak Valley, which I knew never happened, and the time Winston Miller showed up looking for work. Plenty of time for a man who was good at sucking people into his causes to have his face re-done and to make the kind of contacts he'd need to create a new identity. Plenty of time for him to recruit someone in the New York City Police Department to falsify papers. Plenty of time for him to do something about the records of Samuel Towne's incriminating fingerprints. Maybe that wasn't even necessary. Maybe they got rid of dead people's fingerprint records. Plenty of time and plenty of money. You could buy a whole new life with a million dollars.

I'd been making notes whenever something struck me as important. Reading them over, something suddenly struck me as *real* important. Miller became Deputy Chief when Deputy Chief Carl Connigan died in a car accident. Miller became Chief when Chief Geraldo Escondido died in a hunting accident. I've heard of people being accident prone but Winston Miller was benefitting-from-accidents prone. I spent a few minutes thinking about the word *prone*. I thought it meant lying down. Maybe it means you have such a tendency to get into accidents that you can do it lying down.

I realized my mind was wandering and suddenly I felt horribly tired. I wanted to put my head down and go to sleep. I'd probably snore and the guy in the study carrel would bash me on the head with a book. I yawned two or three times, trying to be quiet about it. Then, without even knowing I was going to do it, I suddenly slapped my forehead with the palm of my hand. I ignored the hiss from the carrel.

Why didn't I think of it before? I searched through all the microfiche cassettes, looking for 1969. June 9th. Samuel Towne's picture was on the front page, Samuel Towne with a slightly weak chin, big nose, thin lips firmly closed to hide his crooked teeth, and dark, deep-set eyes, hypnotic eyes, crazy eyes, killer eyes.

I fed a dime into the machine and a photocopy of the page on the screen slid out the side. I found the earliest picture of Winston Miller that was the same size and copied it. I held the two pictures side by side. The noses and chins were different. Miller's ears didn't stick out as much as Towne's and his cheekbones were more prominent. The hairstyles were different, of course. But even with the grainy quality of the copies, there was no mistake: Samuel Towne and Winston Miller had the same eyes.

Chapter Twenty-five

I'd been in the library for over two hours. Before leaving, I checked out *The Art of Horst Martinez*. They had three copies on the shelf, I guess because he's sort of a local-boy-made-good. I sat in the car in the parking lot and read parts of it. Martinez resigned from his teaching job at Oak Valley College in June, 1969, so he could "devote his time to his art." It was three years before he had his first one-man show and "received the recognition his work so richly deserved."

He didn't exactly spend those three years starving in a garret, though. There was a long section describing his house in Los Gatos, where he'd been living and working since August, 1969, having converted the upper floor to a huge studio complete with skylights. Must be nice to be able to quit your job and buy a house. It sure sounded to me like Horst Martinez came into a big hunk of money in the summer of '69, like maybe he received a pay-off for keeping his mouth shut.

I started the car and drove off, not going anywhere in particular, just driving. I saw a phone booth at a gas station, a regular old-fashioned phone booth like Superman used to change his clothes in. Boy, would he have a tough time today when most of the pay phones just hang on a wall. I started giggling, thinking about Clark Kent being arrested for indecent exposure when he dropped his pants outside a 7-11. I pulled up next to the booth and got out of the car.

It took five minutes but he finally came on the line. "Captain Sterling, this is Lizbet Lange. I have to talk to you."

"Where are you?"

"I'm pretty far away." Actually, I was about twelve blocks from the police station. "I need to talk to you."

"Where are you? Do you want me to meet you?"

"Um ..."

"Look, Ms. Lange, I think you're probably pretty confused right now, not sure who you can trust, right?"

"Yeah, something like that."

"Let me tell you what I've been doing. I found out where Mandy Reynolds lives yesterday, but she was on vacation. The San Jose cops knew I was looking for her and they gave me a call this morning. Her neighbor called them because her back door was standing open. The doorknob was broken. Someone broke in, but it didn't look like anything was taken. If he searched the place, he was real careful about it. There was one funny thing though: the answering machine was smashed. Looked like someone put it on the floor and stomped on it. Can't figure that out. Why break into someone's house and smash the answering machine?"

Because when you suddenly realize leaving a message wasn't such a bright idea because voices can be identified and you break in to get rid of the message and you find out someone got there before you, you get so mad you throw the machine on the floor and smash it.

"No ideas, huh? Reason I asked, Ms. Lange, is because your fingerprints are all over Reynolds's apartment."

Oh, *shit.* Shouldn't they have to seal your fingerprints along with your juvie record? *Damn.*

"I was there once, with Amanda's son."

"So I understand. Reynolds has got a gabby neighbor, told me all about Mandy's son the cop. I just got back from your place. Dillon says you were there for just a couple minutes and you were only in the living room. Now how do you suppose your prints got on the phone in the kitchen?"

Damn! Why couldn't Jonathan lie a little and say he gave me the grand tour of his mother's apartment? "What did Amanda say about the x-rays?"

"She's on vacation, I told you. Camping out in Nevada somewhere."

Well, shit. Jonathan could lie through his teeth to protect his mother but couldn't tell a little fib for me. They must have stashed her car in the garage. I was tempted to tell Sterling that Amanda had been right there in my house, just to get even with Jonathan, but I didn't.

"Let me tell you what else I've been working on. I took your boyfriend's advice—"

"He isn't my boyfriend."

"Well, whatever he is. You said I must've told another cop what I was working on. You were right, I did tell someone. Dillon told me to ask him where he was the night Bilbo split."

"What did he say?"

"I didn't ask him. What I did is, I decided to go along with your little scenario, see where it took me. So I talked to the woman who owned your house back in 'sixty-nine. She told me the lawn was put in the morning after Bilbo disappeared. The yard was rototilled or something the day before that. I got hold of the company that did the landscaping. You already know what I found out since your pal Dillon got to Braverman before I did."

"So you know ..."

"I know that a guy who's pretty high up in the police department—a guy who's been a good friend of mine for years—was working for the landscaping company that put the lawn in over those bones in your backyard. That's all I know. Coincidences happen, Ms. Lange, they happen, but I don't like them. Makes me kind of edgy, if things are too coincidental."

"It wasn't a coincidence."

"Maybe not. But that's all I have, and coincidences aren't against the law. So, what I need is something else, some kind of evidence. You happen to have any handy?"

I rested my head against the wall of the booth and tried to think. Should I trust Sterling? Even Charlie lied to me. How could I be sure Sterling was telling the truth? Van Horne was a good friend, he'd said. How good?

"I'll meet you somewhere."

"Okay, where?"

"Robert Martin has to be there, too."

"Who?"

"The FBI guy. Robert Martin."

"Oh, yeah. Okay, no problem. Give me a time and place."

I thought about meeting him at Martin's office, but I didn't really like that idea. I wanted to be someplace where I had more control over things, where I could get away if I needed to. What if Sterling told Martin lies about me and arrested me right there in the FBI office and dragged me off with him? They were both cops and I didn't trust either one of them.

"Ms. Lange?"

"I'm thinking."

"Take your time."

Take your time. I suddenly had a horrible thought: He was tracing the call! Any second now a cop car would pull up and two big squinty-eyed no-necks would drag me off! I hung up

and got in the car and drove away fast, feeling really para-
noid. I kept checking the rearview mirror. I drove around
aimlessly for about thirty minutes, almost wetting my pants
every time I saw a patrol car. Have you ever noticed how
many cops there are just driving around, doing nothing?

I finally stopped at a McDonald's and got a Big Mac and
a cup of coffee. I only ate a couple bites of the hamburger. My
stomach felt really rocky. I decided I had to tell Jonathan what
I'd found out, leaving out the part about Amanda being involved in it. He'd probably figure it out himself when he
found out about the dental records being stashed in her apartment, but I wasn't about to tell him. The pictures of Samuel
Towne and Winston Miller should convince him to believe
me and then he could go with me to see Sterling. I called my
house from the pay phone in the hall by the restrooms. My
answering machine picked the call up. "It's me, Jonathan,
answer the phone."

Nothing happened until the line beeped, signaling the
end of the time I had to leave a message. I called again, and
again the machine answered. "Where are you, Jonathan? I
really need to talk to you. I'll call back in an hour. Um, it's
four-thirty now."

I got another cup of coffee and sat in a booth reading
yesterday's newspaper. I couldn't wait an hour. I called my house
about every ten minutes and got the answering machine every
single time. After the third call, I decided to go home.

I had a horribly uneasy feeling. What if Towne had found
out where they were and he went to my house and Jonathan
and Amanda were lying on the floor with their throats cut
or their heads bashed in? I scared myself so much, I didn't
drive straight home. I went to see Melissa first.

I found her house after only a couple wrong turns. It had

been at least a year since I'd been there. The house was old and saggy and sad-looking. Melissa didn't recognize me at first. I'd forgotten all about my disguise. Once she realized who I was, she didn't seem at all curious about my appearance. Maybe she was just being tactful. "Come on in, Lizbet. Long time no see."

Well, actually it had only been about ten hours. Sometimes I think Melissa doesn't connect with the real world very often. She didn't even blink when I asked her if she knew where I could get a gun.

"What kind, honey? I got a shotgun and a rifle."

"No, a handgun."

"My kid's got a couple thirty-eights. You wanna buy one or what? They aren't registered or nothing like that. He'd probably sell you one. Kid's always short of money. Hey, Matt! Come out here a minute!"

Matt was tall and gangly, the half-Black son of a blonde and a redhead, if you believe Melissa's story. His jeans were hanging off his butt and he was wearing high-top Nikes that made his feet look way too big for him. He had a red baseball cap backward on his head and his hair was past his shoulders, hanging in dark coils.

After he figured out who I was, he told me I looked like shit. I thanked him and told him if I saw him in the mall parking lot at night, I'd run the opposite direction as fast as I could. He seemed to take that as a compliment. He was thrilled to find a buyer for a gun. He probably wanted to get another gold safety pin for his other ear. Or maybe for his nose.

I'd withdrawn four hundred dollars from the bank but I'd spent quite a bit during my shopping spree at K-Mart. I offered him a hundred and fifty. He said, "One seventy-five."

"Does it come with bullets?"

"Sure. I'll throw in some extras, too. Who you gonna shoot?" He grinned, a gold tooth gleaming.

I didn't answer. I gave him the money and Melissa packed the gun and six extra bullets in tissue paper and put them in the biggest shoe box I'd ever seen—size 13. "It's loaded, honey," Melissa said, "so don't point it at anything you don't want to kill."

"I won't. Thanks." I paused at the door. "Um, you won't tell anyone about this, will you?"

They both shook their heads, looking a little surprised that I would even ask. Some people's lives make mine seem almost normal.

Chapter Twenty-six

I drove by my house, then turned around and went back. There were no cars in the driveway. Either Jonathan's car or Amanda's could be in the garage, but not both of them. Mariposa Lane is a winding road with no curbs or sidewalks and no room to park a car on the street, so I turned into my driveway, but instead of following the curve I drove down a gravel path beside the garage, which ends in a wide area where a boat or a motorhome can be parked.

I tucked the shoe box under one arm and grabbed my purse and the tote bag. After turning off the alarm, I opened the storage room door, then went through the connecting door to the garage. The Porsche and the Nova were there. The middle space was empty. I put my purse and the tote bag on a shelf and took the gun out of the shoe box, holding it the way Duke taught me to hold his old twenty-two pistol when he took me out in the desert and let me shoot at tin cans.

I pressed my ear against the door to the kitchen. I didn't hear anything so I unlocked the door and eased it open. After my knees stopped shaking a little, I went in. I'm not sure why I was so nervous. The cars were gone. Obviously Jonathan and Amanda had left. I wasn't going to find their bodies on the floor. Nothing bad had happened here. Still, I tried not to make any noise as I walked through the house, planning to check every room.

The library was the last room downstairs. By then I was used to finding everything the way I left it so I just glanced in and turned away. Then I spun around and walked into the room. I'd been robbed! The display shelves over the bookcases had been stripped of vases and sculptures and statuettes and all those other expensive knickknacks. I stood there staring at the empty shelves, hardly believing what I was seeing, feeling a little sick when I thought of the appraisal form. Close to thirty thousand dollars' worth of stuff and it was all gone.

I was so stunned I stopped worrying about someone being in the house. I went back through the rooms I'd already checked. In the dining room, I opened the doors on the big china cupboard. All the silver was gone—the tea service, the silverware and candlesticks and trays and candy dishes and everything! Five or six thousand dollars worth, at least. Gone!

The crystal miniatures were missing from their display case in the living room. Twenty-five of them, at least, and they cost about a hundred bucks a piece. When I opened the doors to the entertainment center I wasn't even surprised to find that the CD player, VCR, and camcorder were gone. So was an expensive 35-millimeter camera that I hadn't even learned how to use yet. All the CDs were gone, too. Duke and Lady's record collection was still there, which made me feel a little better.

There were little things, little *expensive* things, missing from every room. The big things—televisions, microwaves, stuff like that—hadn't been taken. Everything that was missing could have easily fit into a car. Or two cars.

I went upstairs, pulling myself up with the handrail, feeling really old and tired. My jewelry box was gone. So was the silver dresser tray. I didn't bother trying to figure out what else was missing from the upstairs rooms. I sat on the edge of my bed, holding the gun loosely in my hand. I couldn't even cry.

I don't know how long I sat there, half an hour at least. The phone rang twice but I didn't answer it. I finally called the telephone company. It's all computerized now. You don't have to wait until your bill comes to find out about your toll calls. All you have to do is be really pushy. A woman with a phony nicey-nice voice finally told me that, yes, a call was made at eleven o'clock last night from my phone to the San Jose number I was asking about: Amanda's number.

Amanda had called her apartment to retrieve the messages on her answering machine. Two messages: One from Captain Sterling of the Oak Valley Police Department and one to Clitty-Clitty from Dong-Dong. She knew Sterling had found her and she knew Samuel Towne was alive and up to no good. And then what? Did she tell Jonathan about Towne's threat? She'd have to tell him everything, wouldn't she? All about how she and Charlie planned to steal the money and how she and Towne double-crossed Charlie. And how Towne's message on the answering machine revealed the final double-cross.

I felt really sick when it occurred to me that maybe Jonathan had already known. Maybe she'd told him before, maybe years ago. Maybe the reason he came to Oak Valley when Sterling told him about me wasn't because he wanted to see if his father had been spotted. Maybe he already knew Charlie was dead and he wanted to find out what was going on because if something had turned up, some evidence that his father had been murdered, the whole story might come out.

Amanda hadn't killed anyone herself, but she helped Samuel Towne commit murder and there are laws against that. Conspiracy. Conspiracy to commit murder. Maybe Jonathan came to Oak Valley to find out if his mother was in danger of being exposed as an accomplice in the murder of his father. When I practically dropped into his lap, he might have decided his best bet was to keep an eye on me and find out what I was up to. He hadn't been eager for me to go to the FBI or talk to Sterling. I remembered him walking around my house like a prospective buyer, checking everything out. Had it already occurred to him that they might have to run? Had he already been deciding what he'd take, mentally adding up the value of all my pretty things? He was a cop. He probably knew a good fence. What a liar! Just like Charlie. Like father, like son.

"Charlie? Can you come back?" I didn't even realize I was going to say the words until they popped out of my mouth. I tingled and Charlie appeared in front of me.

"Please don't do that again, Lizbet. I know you're mad at me, but sending me away isn't going to help. What are you doing with a gun?"

I glared at him. "Your stupid cow of a wife ripped me off, Charlie, and I think your precious son is a liar and a thief, too."

"Ex-wife. What's Jonathan done?"

"Widow. They stole my silver and all my jewelry and a whole bunch of other stuff. Thousands and thousands of dollars worth of stuff. *My* stuff."

"Hmmm. What are you doing with a gun?"

"Nothing."

"Well, why don't you put it down and tell me what else has happened."

"I don't want to put it down. I'm thinking about shooting you. You got me into this mess. I didn't mind so much when I thought you were a nice guy who got killed, but you weren't. You got exactly what you deserved."

"The death penalty. I was always in favor of it. I've paid for my sins, Lizbet, or at least for my crimes. Besides, you can't shoot me, I'm already dead. Why is your hair brown?"

"I like it brown. Maybe I'll shoot Jonathan instead."

"Are you sure he stole your things? Why would he?"

"To help Amanda. She must have told him the whole story and they robbed me so she'd have enough money to get away. Samuel Towne's after her, too."

"Towne's alive? Well, well. How'd you find out?"

I filled him in, telling him about the message on Amanda's machine and the hours I spent at the library. I also told him about Horst Martinez, which reminded me that I should listen to the news to see if he was dead. I put the gun on the nightstand and tuned the clock radio to the local all-news station. The announcer was talking about the stock market.

"I don't understand why Towne would want to be a police chief, Charlie. It can't pay all that much. Do you suppose he just thought it was a good joke?"

"He's probably involved in half the crime in the state. All he'd need is a reliable go-between so the crooks don't know who they're really working for. Listen."

While the announcer read the story we both stared at the radio, like we thought it was really a television. I didn't kill Horst Martinez after all. He was in serious but stable condition after suffering his third heart attack in five years. He was an old pro at it.

"Feel better?" Charlie asked. I did, sort of, at least. I was so relieved I felt shaky, but it did occur to me that if he had died he wouldn't ever be able to tell anyone that I was the one who shocked him into having a heart attack. Oh, well, maybe he'd never figure out who I was. I turned off the radio.

"What should I do, Charlie? Trust Sterling? And what am I going to do about Jonathan? I should call the cops and report the burglary but ..."

"Theft. They didn't break in."

"Oh, stop being a cop, Charlie. I don't care what it's called, they still stole all my stuff."

"Are you sure Jonathan's involved? Seems to me he'd tell Amanda to get a good lawyer. It's been a lot of years. The only real evidence against her is the dental records being found in her apartment and I'm not sure if they'd carry much weight in court, especially since you removed them. Lawyers have a way of getting evidence suppressed if there's a chance it's been tampered with. Same with the answering machine tape. I think Amanda's probably more afraid of Samuel Towne than the law."

"So where's Jonathan?"

"Looking for his mother, maybe, or looking for you."

I thought about that for a minute, then said, "The phone rang."

"I didn't hear anything."

"Not now. A little while ago. It rang twice."

I went downstairs to the casual living room, Charlie right on my heels. The answering machine light was blinking. Nobody ever calls me so I'm not used to checking it.

There weren't just two messages, there were twelve. Five of them were the calls I'd made from McDonald's trying to get hold of Jonathan. Captain Sterling had called twice, asking me to get in touch with him. The others were from Jonathan. I got all weak in the knees when I heard his voice.

His first message was short: *It's me. You weren't burglarized, so don't call the cops, okay? My mother ... I'll explain it later. She left me a note ...* He didn't say anything else, but I could hear him breathing until his time was up and the machine clicked off. I was breathing kind of funny myself and I had to keep blinking back tears. He wasn't just another loser, after all. Charlie was watching me very intently and I sure wished he'd stop.

Jonathan must have called right back because the second message started where the first one left off: *Me, again. She told me the x-rays were at her apartment, but I've been there and they're gone. The cops've been there, too. Someone broke in last night.* After a second, just before the machine cut him off, he added: *She said Towne's after her. I don't understand what's going on. He's supposed to be dead.*

I understood exactly what was going on and I sure felt bad for Jonathan. "God, Charlie, he's known for years that you're no good and now his mother turns out to be rotten, too. I'm surprised he hasn't gone completely off the deep end. I hope you're ashamed of yourself."

Charlie shushed me impatiently as the third message started: *I just talked to her bank. Being a cop is handy sometimes.* He sighed, then added: *She cleared out her checking account and savings account.* He didn't say anything else, but he didn't hang up until the machine beeped either.

The fourth message was: *I tried to get hold of her friends at the RV camp but they aren't there. The manager said he'd tell her to call me if she shows up, but ... maybe I'd better head to Reno.*

The last time he called, he said: *Dammit, Lizbet, where are you?* After a pause, he added: *Look, I'm sorry about your things. I was awake half the night worrying about what you were up to and I took a nap this afternoon. She was gone when I woke up.*

"Some cop," I said to Charlie. "She carted off half the house practically from right under his nose."

Charlie grinned. *"Why don't you call him? He's probably worried about you."*

I called, but got his machine. I just said, "Call me," and hung up.

"Now," said Charlie, *"let's figure out how to get this mess cleared up."*

Chapter Twenty-seven

We went upstairs to see if Jonathan had left his briefcase. I checked Amanda's room first. There was nothing of hers in it and there were some things of mine that weren't in it, the bitch. She'd left the bed unmade. I hate unmade beds but I didn't feel like touching the sheets she'd slept on, or even looking at them, so I went on to Jonathan's room.

His bed was neatly made. I wondered who taught him. It sure hadn't been Amanda. Suzanne the Wonder Cop? I thought he'd taken everything with him at first, but the suitcase and briefcase were in the closet. I opened the briefcase and found the picture of Charlie and Amanda and little Jonathan in their backyard. After getting the gun from my bedroom, we went back downstairs.

I retrieved my purse and the shoe box and tote bag from the garage. After packing the gun away, I emptied the tote bag on the kitchen table. Charlie asked about the x-rays Pete had given me at the morgue, so I got them from the drawer where I'd stashed them. They matched Charlie's x-rays from Amanda's files.

"The x-rays Sterling showed you will match Ivan Kosvak's. Two identical sets with different names on them. That should convince the cops someone tampered with the x-rays. This is looking good. What else?"

"Well, we have the photograph of you wearing the peace

symbol the day before you died and we have the picture in the art book showing Horst Martinez wearing the same pendant twenty years later."

"Which implicates Martinez. The condition he's in, he might be in the mood for a deathbed confession."

"Here's the biggie," I said and handed him the two photocopies I'd made at the library. He took them—ghost copies of them—and I put the real copies down. "What do you think? Same eyes, right?"

He was smiling happily at the pictures. *"Same eyes. Definitely. It's really him."*

"You know, once Sterling sees this stuff I don't think he's really going to care how I got involved in it. He probably won't even ask how I came up with your name."

"Maybe not, but we still need an explanation."

"But I can't think of one. I don't think it matters, Charlie. I can't explain how I knew you had a bridge either, but I guess I could get away with a lie. The swimming pool guys came and got me as soon as they dug you up. I can just claim I took a good look then. No one can prove I didn't, even if I did act a little squeamish about getting near the bones after the cops got here."

"That should work, but we still need to explain how you knew my name."

"I don't see why—"

"Come with me."

I followed him into the casual living room. He opened the sliding glass door and stepped outside. I opened the sliding glass door—the real one—and joined him on the patio. He looked around, then said, *"Over there, I think."* I followed him to a section of the yard that's covered with ice plant. Ice plant is a succulent herb that makes a great low-maintenance ground cover although you wouldn't want to walk on the ground it's covering because the leaves are so thick. It was in bloom, full of bright purple and pink blossoms.

"Pull that out," Charlie said. He was pointing to a piece of ice plant that was brown and shriveled. I frowned at it. It hadn't been much more than a week since the yard maintenance people Tom had hired came by and they do a real good job. I'd never noticed any dead ice plant before. The stuff grows like a weed and doesn't need to be babied at all. You have to keep cutting it back or it'll take over the whole yard. I yanked up the dying plant. Big clods of dirt clung to the roots.

"See it?" Charlie was pointing at the ground. Sticking partly out of the dirt was something brown and square. Mother Nature doesn't make square things. I plucked it out and brushed off the loose dirt. It was a flat leather case, like the ones for credit cards, but square instead of rectangular. The leather was cracked and rotting and felt damp. Inside was Charlie's police identification card, which was laminated in heavy plastic and didn't look too bad for having spent twenty-seven years under the ground.

I looked at Charlie. "How did you know it was there?"

"I always carried my ID card, but I had to be sure no one accidentally saw it. Amanda stitched a small pocket inside the waistband of my jeans for it. It must have fallen out while they were carrying my body. You found it, a few days before the bones turned up. You knew it was old, but you wanted to try to return it to the owner. There was no Charlie Bilbo in the phone book, so you called the police department. You don't remember who you talked to, but whoever it was told you Charlie Bilbo disappeared after killing some other cops in nineteen sixty-nine. You were curious so you went to the library and read all about it."

"And when the bones turned up, I was sure they had to be yours. That'll work, won't it?"

"Sure. And you wouldn't tell the cops because you were afraid you'd get in trouble for not turning the ID card over to them when you first found it. Besides, they acted funny when you mentioned my name. You're young. They'll believe you."

"And I wouldn't tell Sterling later on because I was sure a cop was involved and I didn't know if I could trust him. Okay. Charlie, has it really been there all this time?"

He just smiled.

"They didn't find an ID card with your bones. Amanda would have told Samuel Towne where you kept it. He would have cut it to pieces or burned it or something. It couldn't have been there all these years." Charlie didn't say anything. "What if Towne tells the cops he destroyed it?"

"Who will believe him?"

I rubbed my finger across the leather case, making little bits of leather flake off. "I thought you didn't have any magic powers, like making police IDs appear out of thin air."

He shrugged. *"I think you should call Sterling now. Meet him somewhere. Insist on having the FBI agent there if that makes you feel safer, although Sterling seems to be in the clear. I don't think you'll have any trouble convincing him. You said he's already suspicious of Van Horne."*

"Aren't you coming with me?"

"I have to leave now." He smiled, that glorious Charlie Bilbo smile. *"It's been nice knowing you, Lizbet."*

I stepped toward him, reaching out to touch him but drawing my hand back quickly. "No! Wait, Charlie! Don't leave yet. It isn't over yet."

"My part is over. I have a gift for you." He raised his right hand, index and middle finger extended in a V, and he said two words and then he was gone.

"Charlie! Come back!"

Nothing happened. Well, phooey. And what gift?

Chapter Twenty-eight

It was almost seven o'clock so I didn't really expect Captain Sterling to be at the police department, but he was. "I thought you'd have gone home already," I said.

"I've forgotten where I live by now, Ms. Lange. Why did you hang up on me?"

"I don't know. I just changed my mind."

"I see. And why are you calling this time?"

"I have some stuff for you. Evidence."

"I see. Evidence of what?"

"Charlie's murder, stuff like that."

"What kind of evidence?"

"I have the dental x-rays."

"You do? Where did you find them? Ah, of course, in Mandy Reynolds's apartment. Why would she keep all those old files? Mrs. Yakamoto seemed pretty sure they'd been thrown out."

"She only kept the important ones."

"I see. Why did you smash the answering machine?"

"I didn't. Samuel Towne did that."

"Samuel Towne? He's been dead for almost thirty years, Ms. Lange."

"He's baaa-aack."

Sterling didn't say anything.

"Meet me by the fountain at Oak Valley Mall in an hour. Bring Robert Martin with you. If he isn't there, I won't talk to you."

"Wait! Don't hang up!"

But I did.

The way Sterling kept saying *I see* made me pretty sure he thought he was dealing with a real nut-case. Well, he didn't know what I knew, did he?

It's only a twenty-minute drive to the mall, but I wanted to get out of the house. As soon as Charlie left, I started feeling nervous, thinking about Samuel Towne and Theodore Van Horne being out there somewhere. I rummaged around in the tote bag for my sunglasses and stuck them on top of my head so I'd have them handy. Sunglasses always make you feel anonymous. I'd just be one more cokehead hangin' at the mall. I almost trusted Sterling, but why take chances? I wanted to get close enough to be sure Robert Martin was with him before he spotted me, just in case.

I picked up the tote bag and my purse. The shoe box was right beside them. Take it or leave it? I only bought the gun because I was afraid to come in the house without it, but I decided to take it with me anyway, for the same reason I wanted the sunglasses: just in case.

I went out the back way through the garage and storage room. The sun was setting, streaking the sky with bright pink. I backed the rental car down the gravel drive toward the front of the house. When the car cleared the front wall of the house, I hit the brake so hard I almost gave myself whiplash. A dark blue sedan was parked in the circular drive. Two men were standing beside it, staring at me. I felt like I was going to be joining Horst Martinez in the coronary care unit real soon.

Deputy Chief of Police Theodore Van Horne and his

boss, Chief of Police Winston Miller. The man with Samuel Towne's eyes. Coming toward me. Oh, my god!

I yanked the sunglasses down over my eyes and poked my head out the window as they came around the car to the driver's side. "Are you looking for Lizbet? She isn't home."

"Who are you?"

"Melissa O'Neal. Lizbet used to work with me down at Tony's Truck Stop before she got rich, you know? Her ex left her a ton of money. Some people have all the luck, huh? I come up here and work for her, do ironing, sew buttons on, stuff like that. She isn't home."

Winston Miller said, "Step out of the car, please."

"Huh?"

He flipped open a little brown case like Charlie's and showed me a gold shield with *Chief of Police* on it.

"Hey, what is this? Lizbet gave me a key and everything. I didn't do anything wrong."

"Get out of the car."

I thought of all the stuff in the tote bag: the x-rays, the answering machine tape, the pictures of Samuel Towne and Winston Miller, Charlie's police ID. All the evidence. "Okay, okay," I said and reached for my purse, jerking the strap up on my shoulder. "Jeez, I haven't done anything wrong."

I moved the gear shift, sliding it from Reverse to Park then right back to Reverse, hoping Miller wasn't watching too carefully. I unhooked my seatbelt and reached for the door handle. When Miller stepped back to give me room to open the door, I took my foot off the brake and floored the accelerator. The car roared down the drive, more or less heading for the street. I only looked back long enough to aim the car, then I jerked my head around to see what Miller and

Van Horne were doing. Van Horne had his gun out but Miller grabbed his arm and they both ran toward their car.

I felt the tires leave the pavement and looked back to see where I was, yanking the wheel hard to the right just in time to miss the mailbox. The car shot backward into the street. I didn't even see the other car. I just smashed right into it. Since I'd taken my seatbelt off, the impact threw me against the steering wheel and I felt all the air go out of my body. I didn't pass out, though. I think there was so much adrenaline rushing through my veins by then that it would have taken a massive dose of sedatives to knock me out. The sunglasses were hanging from my left ear. I shook them off and shoved the lid off the shoebox and grabbed the gun and got out of the car.

"*Lizbet!*"

Jesus, it was Jonathan. I'd smashed in the whole front end of his car. "Oh, god, Jonathan, it's him, it's him!" I was jumping up and down and pointing wildly toward my house, waving the gun around like a crazy woman. Miller and Van Horne were trotting down the driveway toward me.

"Give me that gun. What are you doing with a gun? You're hurt—"

I slapped his hand away. I knew I was hurt, for crying out loud, there was blood all over my hands and I could feel it dripping down my face. My nose felt like someone hammered it flat. "It's *Samuel Towne,* Jonathan!"

"Stop waving that gun around, Lizbet. Are you nuts? What the hell did you do to your hair?"

"It's *him,*" I hissed at Jonathan. He put his arm around my shoulders and whispered, "Van Horne won't do anything. That's the Chief of Police with him."

I jerked away from him. He let go of me, but somehow he managed to twist the gun out of my hand. "You idiot!" I

stomped my foot at him and spun around to face Samuel
Towne, vaguely aware that people—neighbors—were running
toward the wreck. Safety in numbers. I suddenly felt a lot
calmer. Samuel Towne couldn't very well kill me right in front
of Jonathan and a dozen other people right there on Mariposa Lane, could he? Someone shouted something about an
ambulance.

"I don't want an ambulance," I said to Jonathan. "I *like*
my hair brown."

"You're hurt, Ms. Lange. It is Ms. Lange, isn't it?" Samuel
Towne was smiling at me, flashing Winston Miller's perfect teeth.

"I know who you are," I said.

"Yes, of course. I told you who I am," he said soothingly,
then he looked at Jonathan. "I showed her my shield and she
panicked. Don't I know you?"

"Jonathan Dillon, sir. I'm with the San Jose Police."
Jonathan shook his hand! I couldn't believe it.

I grabbed Jonathan's arm, shaking it. "You have to listen
to me! I have proof. I have—"

"Why don't we get Ms. Lange into the house?" Towne
said. "She should probably lie down."

Jonathan had his arm around me again and tried to steer
me toward the house. I pulled away so hard I almost fell down.
I wanted to stay right out there in the middle of the street. I
suddenly realized Van Horne was missing. I spotted him standing by his car, talking on a cellular telephone.

I had a flash of insight so strong it was like the top of my
head came off. Samuel Towne was in control here, in control
of the police department and in control of other things,
darker things, criminal things. If I got in an ambulance, I'd
be dead before I got to the hospital, or right after I got there.

That's what Van Horne was doing on the phone, setting things up, arranging for the right people to come get me or to be at the hospital when I was brought in.

I grabbed Jonathan's arm again, shaking it frantically. "Don't do anything he says. Don't let them take me away, Jonathan. He's Samuel Towne. I can prove it."

Jonathan looked confused, which I guess was understandable, but I was getting panicky and knew it would take more time than I had to explain it to him. I could hear an ambulance siren in the distance, getting louder every second. I glanced at the group of people who'd come out of their houses. None of them knew who I was. They were too well-bred to sneer, but I knew they saw a hysterical woman wearing flashy clothes and too much makeup. They all knew who Winston Miller was. He was on television all the time. They wouldn't question anything he did.

Samuel Towne was leaning into my car through the driver's side window. Oh, my god, the evidence! He straightened up, my tote bag in his hand. I turned to Jonathan. He was holding my gun loosely, his hand curled around it. When I grabbed for it, he said, "For god's sake, Lizbet, are you crazy?" and raised his arm, holding the gun out of my reach.

I dropped to my knees and fumbled at his pants leg. It took him just a half-second too long to realize what I was doing. Just as he reached down and grabbed my shoulder, I pulled the gun out of his ankle holster and spun around on my knees, my pants ripping against the asphalt. I brought the gun up, aiming at Samuel Towne, who was only a yard away. I heard a hissing intake of air from the crowd of gawkers.

"You put that bag down," I said.

Towne said, "Shoot her."

I thought he was talking to Jonathan at first, then I caught a movement out of the corner of my eye and knew Van Horne was at my side.

Jonathan said, "No! Lizbet, put the gun down."

"Shoot her," Towne said.

I heard Jonathan's shoes scraping against the pavement and then he said, "Pull the trigger and you're dead, Van Horne."

A woman in the crowd shrieked, the sound cut off abruptly, like someone had clamped a hand over her mouth. There wasn't a sound from the crowd after that. We must have been quite a sight, the four of us almost within arm's length of each other, me on my knees pointing a gun at the Chief of Police, Van Horne pointing a gun at me, Jonathan pointing at gun at him. Talk about a vicious circle!

An ambulance screamed around the last curve of the road and rolled to stop. I didn't hear any doors open. I guess the paramedics weren't all that eager to walk into the middle of a shoot-out. The last of the sunlight was fading fast but the ambulance headlights were aimed at us, bathing us in bright light.

The gun was starting to feel awfully heavy. "Put the bag down," I said to Towne, who was squinting against the light. "Put it on the hood of the car."

He didn't move. At least he'd stopped telling Van Horne to shoot me. Maybe he wasn't sure his Deputy Chief was willing to die for him.

"Do it," Jonathan said, in a cop voice that would have scared me if he'd been talking to me.

Towne hesitated, then put the tote bag on the hood of the Ford. "The woman is hysterical, Dillon. For god's sake, get the gun away from her."

I heard Jonathan moving. The gun was so heavy my

arms were shaking. It was taking all my concentration to keep it aimed at Towne. Jonathan came into sight as he backed up to my car, keeping his gun on Van Horne. He reached behind him with his left hand and got the tote bag. "Put the gun down, Van Horne. Sterling knows you were working for Braverman when Charlie Bilbo was killed. It's all going to come out. Put the gun down."

There were sirens—a zillion of them from the sound—coming up Foothill Avenue. The ambulance driver must have radioed for help. Towne glanced in that direction, his face looking blanched in the bright glow of the headlights. I couldn't see Van Horne but he must have laid his gun down because Jonathan disappeared from my sight for a moment, then Van Horne walked over and stood beside Towne. Jonathan was at my side, a gun in each hand, covering Towne and Van Horne. He looked like the good guy in a cowboy movie, except for the silly tote bag hanging on his arm. "Relax, Lizbet," he said.

I sat back on my heels and lowered the gun, resting my hands on my knees, ready to bring the gun back up if Towne moved.

"I'll have your badge for this, Dillon."

"Maybe you will, Miller, but Lizbet hasn't been wrong yet so I think I'll wait and see what she has to show us."

The sirens were screaming. "Jonathan, they'll be on his side. They won't believe me." I tried to get to my feet, but didn't have the strength. Three or four cars screeched to a stop and doors slammed and I heard people running. I tugged on Jonathan's pants leg, saying, "We have to get hold of Sterling. I told him to meet me at the mall."

"I was on my way, Ms. Lange, when I heard all the commotion over the radio. Thought I'd better come see what was going on." Sterling leaned down and helped me to my feet.

Robert Martin, the FBI guy, was talking to Jonathan, who handed him the guns. I wobbled over to him and got the tote bag, wrapping both my arms around it, hugging it against my chest. Jonathan took his gun out of my hand and put an arm around my shoulders.

It looked like every cop in the world was on Mariposa Lane, most of them standing in a semicircle around me and Jonathan and Sterling and Towne and Van Horne, like we were putting on a play and they were the audience. Samuel Towne said, "This woman's insane, John."

Sterling smiled, the meanest cop smile I've ever seen. "Maybe she is, Winston. She does come up with the craziest ideas. Like how it couldn't just be a coincidence that Van Horne was working for the landscaping company that put grass over a grave in her backyard. And like how I should find out who hired Bill Colton to tail her. When I asked Colton how the surveillance was going, he figured I knew all about it. Talkative guy, Colton, especially if you buy him a drink or two. He also told me he hadn't been able to locate Mandy Reynolds yet. Another little job you hired him to do. Oh, yeah, and he mentioned how he sure felt bad about having to hit Betty Yakamoto over the head when she showed up unexpectedly."

Sweat was pouring down Samuel Towne's face. Van Horne looked like he'd given up completely and was trying to go back to the womb. He was slumped against the fender of my car, all bent over and weak-looking. I felt the way he looked. If I hadn't been leaning against Jonathan, I probably would have fallen over.

"You know what Ms. Lange's latest crazy idea is, Winston? She says she has evidence that Samuel Towne's still alive. Seeing as how I've been wondering myself if that was really him who died back in 'sixty-nine, I'm real curious about what she has to show me. Maybe it'll explain why you've been trying to beat me to the dental records."

"He's Samuel Towne," I said. "Winston Miller. He's really Samuel Towne. It's all in my bag." Then I took Lady's advice and pulled the fragile-female trick. I found out later that Jonathan caught me before I hit the ground.

Chapter Twenty-nine

It's been a week now and things are starting to settle down. The brown stuff washed right out of my hair and the doctor says my nose will be just as cute as ever once the swelling goes down and the bruises fade. The Splash 'N Shine guys are back at work and I'll be able to swim in my very own swimming pool this summer.

Sterling says it'll probably take months for them to figure out all the criminal activity Samuel Towne was mixed up in, if they ever do. As Winston Miller, Chief of Police, he made Oak Valley a nice low-crime city, mainly by running out all his competitors and confining his own criminal operations to San Francisco and Los Angeles. The cops are investigating the supposedly accidental deaths of Carl Connigan and Geraldo Escondido, which led to Winston Miller's promotion to Deputy Chief and then Chief. The New York City Police Department confirmed that Winston Miller's employment records were forged.

Sterling didn't have any trouble believing I found Charlie's ID card and jumped to the conclusion that the bones were his and was afraid to tell the cops how I knew. So the big mystery of how I knew those were Charlie's bones has been solved.

Samuel Towne is still refusing to talk. I don't mean that

he just won't waive his rights. He completely refuses to say a word to anybody, including his own lawyer. He won't write anything down or even nod or shake his head. He's also on a hunger strike.

Theodore Van Horne committed suicide right after I passed out on Mariposa Lane. He was carrying a second gun, a derringer, and he stuck it in his mouth and pulled the trigger before anyone could stop him. From something Jonathan said, I think maybe they could have stopped him if they hadn't all been acting like a bunch of chickens with their heads cut off because I'd fainted on them. Men! Well, mostly men; one of the cops was a woman and I guess she wasn't any calmer than the rest of them. Jeez, you'd think they'd never seen a woman faint before. But I'm not going to feel guilty about no one noticing what Van Horne was up to. I'm just glad I was out cold when he blew his brains out.

Horst Martinez is still in the hospital. I told Sterling how I caused his heart attack and he thought it was really funny, so I guess I'm not going to get in any trouble. Martinez had dabbled in radical politics at Oak Valley College and knew Samuel Towne then. I was wrong about him getting the money for his house from Towne, though. He inherited it from his grandmother. He wasn't involved at all until Towne came back to Oak Valley and started getting his picture in the paper on a regular basis. With his artist's eye for detail, Martinez recognized him right away. Towne gave him some money and the peace symbol in exchange for his silence. If he hadn't been wearing the peace symbol when a photographer snapped his picture unexpectedly, no one ever would have known he was involved. He's known for years that Winston Miller and Samuel Towne were one and the same, so he'll be in big trouble if he survives heart surgery next week.

Amanda has vanished completely. About the same time all the commotion was going on in front of my house, she showed up in Reno. She took her Winnebago away from her friends who were vacationing in it, sold the motorhome to an RV dealer, and disappeared. I reported the theft so the insurance will cover it, but Sterling says I'll probably never get my stuff back if she's smart and sells it a piece or two at a time in other states. Jonathan says I should redo the library shelves with art that reflects my own personality. I don't know what that means. Bronzed editions of *The National Enquirer?* Still-lifes of cheeseburgers and Chinese take-out? A bust of Kurt Cobain? Maybe I'll collect hippie memorabilia—sort of a tribute to Duke and Lady.

Jonathan's doing pretty good, all things considered. He was heading out of town, planning to drive to Reno to look for his mother, when he stopped at a pay phone to check for messages on his answering machine one more time. As soon as he heard my message saying "Call me," he hurried to my place, which is how he happened to show up when he did. When I woke up at the hospital, after sleeping about twelve hours, he was sitting beside my bed, holding my hand. He's pretty shook up about his mother and I haven't seen much of him, but we talk on the phone every day, mostly about things that aren't very important, but as soon as he's feeling better I'm going to make him tell me why he came to my room the night I slipped out to go to Amanda's apartment. He told me that's how he found out I was gone, but he skipped right over his reason for being in my bedroom in the middle of the night. I'm just kind of curious, you know?

So anyway, Jonathan's feeling pretty bad right now, but I think he'll be okay. He's lost his mother, but in a way he got his father back. You see, Horst Martinez doesn't know the whole story and Amanda's missing and Van Horne's dead and Towne isn't talking, so I'm the only one who could tell him the truth.

Sterling pieced the story together from what facts he had. The way he figures it, Amanda and Samuel Towne became lovers and plotted to steal the money. They switched the x-rays so Kosvak's body would be identified as Towne, then blew up the warehouse while Kosvak was inside, not knowing the SWAT team was about to make its move. They murdered Charlie, burying his body where it would never be found so everyone would think he was responsible for stealing the money and blowing up the building. Then, of course, Towne skipped out on Amanda.

I know the truth, but I can't tell anyone because there's no earthly explanation for my knowing that Charlie stole the money and rigged the bomb to kill Kosvak and Towne and that he only ended up dead himself because Amanda double-crossed him. Amanda knows the truth, but she's gone and I don't think she'll ever come back. Towne knows the truth, but he isn't talking and even if he does I don't think anyone will believe him. So, for now at least, Charlie is a hero, a good cop, an innocent man who was murdered and falsely accused. The headlines read: COP'S NAME CLEARED AFTER TWENTY-SEVEN YEARS.

Pretty soon, that's what I'll believe, too, because it's all slipping away. At first, I thought I was just getting confused because I had to answer hundreds of questions and tell the same story over and over. I thought that was why I would suddenly realize I'd forgotten all about Charlie being here. The more often I told the story, the more it seemed that it really did happen that way, that I really did find his ID card in my yard before his bones turned up, that Charlie was never here. I thought it was just because I was tired, but now I know it isn't. My memory of Charlie is getting weaker and weaker, and my "memory" of the story I told the cops is getting stronger and stronger. In a few more days I won't remember Charlie being here at all.

There's no earthly explanation for a ghost. My memory of him is just one more loose end that Charlie had to tie up. That's the gift he gave me just before he left, when he raised his hand, his index and middle finger extended in a V, and said: *"Peace, Lizbet."*